The
DEMON SWORD MASTER
of Excalibur Academy

REGINA

Riselia's personal maid. An expert at spoiling people.

LEONIS(?)

Riselia's strict and demanding drill sergeant. In actuality, he's...

"Haah, haah, haah... I can still keep going!"

RISELIA
Leonis's minion and guardian. Overprotective.

RIVAIZ

The Lord of the Seas.
One of the eight
Dark Lords.

"Maybe you
should start
minding
them, then."

LEONIS

The strongest Dark Lord.
He was reincarnated
into the body of a ten-
year-old boy.

"The great dragons don't mind little details like that!"

VEIRA

The proud Dragon Lord. She was resurrected after a thousand years.

"Bothersome insects. Leave my sight at once."

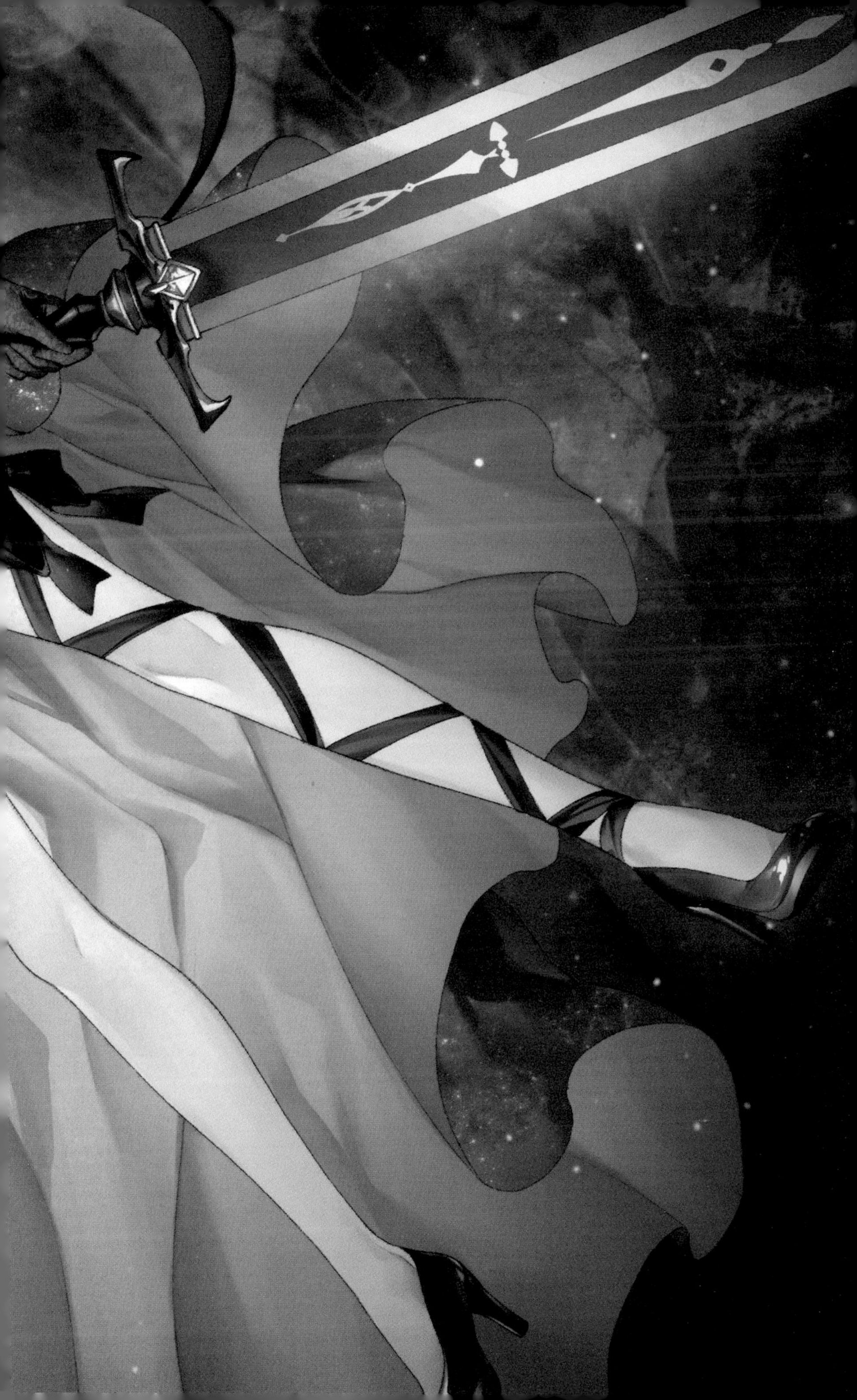

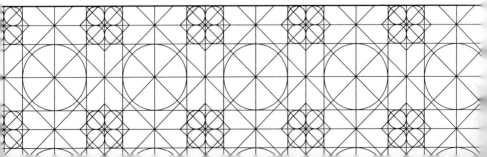

Contents

The Demon Sword Master of Excalibur Academy

The DEMON SWORD MASTER of Excalibur Academy

[**8**]

Yu Shimizu

ILLUSTRATION

Asagi Tohsaka

YEN ON

NEW YORK

The Demon Sword Master of Excalibur Academy

Yu Shimizu

Translation by Roman Lempert
Cover art by Asagi Tohsaka

SEIKEN GAKUIN NO MAKEN TSUKAI Volume 8
©Yu Shimizu 2021
First published in Japan in 2021 by KADOKAWA CORPORATION, Tokyo.
English translation rights arranged with KADOKAWA CORPORATION, Tokyo, through TUTTLE-MORI AGENCY, INC., Tokyo.

English translation © 2023 by Yen Press, LLC

Yen On
150 West 30th Street, 19th Floor
New York, NY 10001

Visit us at yenpress.com
facebook.com/yenpress ★ twitter.com/yenpress
yenpress.tumblr.com ★ instagram.com/yenpress

First Yen On Edition: April 2023
Edited by Yen On Editorial: Jordan Blanco
Designed by Yen Press Design: Liz Parlett

Yen On is an imprint of Yen Press, LLC.
The Yen On name and logo are trademarks of Yen Press, LLC.

The publisher is not responsible for websites (or their content) that are not owned by the publisher.

Library of Congress Cataloging-in-Publication Data
Names: Shimizu, Yu, author. | Tohsaka, Asagi, illustrator. | Lempert, Roman, translator.
Title: The demon sword master of Excalibur Academy / Yu Shimizu ; illustration by Asagi Tohsaka ; translation by Roman Lempert.
Other titles: Seiken gakuin no maken tsukai. English
Description: First Yen On edition. | New York : Yen On, 2020.
Identifiers: LCCN 2020017005 | ISBN 9781975308667 (v. 1 ; trade paperback) |
ISBN 9781975319151 (v. 2 ; trade paperback) | ISBN 9781975320706 (v. 3 ; trade paperback) |
ISBN 9781975320720 (v. 4 ; trade paperback) | ISBN 9781975335427 (v. 5 ; trade paperback) |
ISBN 9781975343460 (v. 6 ; trade paperback) | ISBN 9781975343484 (v. 7 ; trade paperback) |
ISBN 9781975348625 (v. 8 ; trade paperback)
Subjects: CYAC: Fantasy. | Demonology—Fiction. | Reincarnation—Fiction
Classification: LCC PZ7.1.S5174 De 2020 | DDC [Fic]—dc23
LC record available at https://lccn.loc.gov/2020017005

ISBNs: 978-1-9753-4862-5 (paperback)
978-1-9753-4863-2 (ebook)

10 9 8 7 6 5 4 3 2 1

LSC-C

Printed in the United States of America

The Demon Sword Master of Excalibur Academy

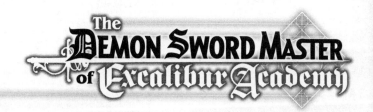

Characters

Riselia

A girl who became Leonis's minion and, at the same time, his guardian.

Leonis

The Undead King and greatest Dark Lord. Was reborn after a thousand years, but for some reason, he ended up in the form of a ten-year-old boy.

Regina

Riselia's personal maid. Harboring a secret.

Sakuya

A girl from the Sakura Orchid, a place ravaged by the Voids. A master swordswoman.

Elfiné

Operator of Leonis's platoon. Heiress of the Phillet Company.

Shary

An assassin maid. One of Leonis's dark minions. Loves sweets.

Blackas

One of Leonis's dark minions and prince of the Realm of Shadows. Very fluffy.

Veira

The Dragon Lord excavated from the northern tundra. Like Leonis, she is a Dark Lord.

CHAPTER 1

DUKE CRYSTALIA

The Azure Hold floated over the seas, casting its massive shadow upon the raging waves. And hovering in the empty air above the Dragon Lord's stronghold was a man. A white-haired hero, clad in military uniform, his hawklike, ice-blue eyes glaring down at Leonis and Veira, who stood on the remains of the leviathan.

…Why would this man be here?!

Leonis scowled because he recognized this man. He'd seen a picture of him in the estate amid the ruins of the Third Assault Garden.

Edward Ray Crystalia. Riselia's dad, who had supposedly perished in battle with the Voids.

Isn't her father dead? More importantly, why's he here? Questions filled Leonis's mind, but he couldn't conjure any answers.

"I'm surprised you have the nerve to show yourself before me again," the crimson dragon beside Leonis snarled. "You have courage. I grant you that much."

Veira's furious roar shook the air violently, but the man floating above didn't seem at all troubled by the palpable waves of a Dark Lord's fury beating against him.

Was he the one who mentally dominated Veira…?

Even if the Dragon Lord was careless, no ordinary human could control a Dark Lord's mind.

What is he? Just who is Duke Crystalia...? Leonis cautiously observed the man overhead.

"So you've returned, Veira Greater Dragon. How fortuitous." The man resembling Duke Crystalia eyed the Dragon Lord coldly. Then he pointed an index finger at a spot between her eyes.

"Holy Sword, Wheel of Fortune—Activate."

Light gathered at his fingertip...

"Veira!" Leonis exclaimed.

"The same trick again? You underestimate the Dragon Lord!"

Incandescent, white-hot flames issued from Veira's maw, becoming a surging blade of heat.

Bwoooooooosh!

The air trembled. The flames swallowed the man in an instant and then went on to incinerate the walls of the Azure Hold behind him.

"Oh, did I reduce him to ashes?"

"F-fool, show some restraint! There's much we need to ask him!" Leonis shouted.

And then...

Crack...

"...?!"

...Leonis heard cracking glass.

"It's you who underestimates me, Dragon Lord."

A fissure ran through the space before the pair of Dark Lords, and the man appeared from within, unharmed. His expression was composed, and there wasn't a single burn on his uniform.

"Gravity-type, eighth-order spell—Veira Zarga." The man suddenly chanted a spell.

Did he just use sorcery?!

Leonis quickly formed a tower shield from his shadow.

Vroom, brrrrrrrrrrr!

A lump of gravity, akin to that of a giant planet, hit Veira directly.

...An eighth-order gravity spell... Leonis pondered calmly behind his shield.

As far as Leonis knew, the ancient, powerful ways of magic were an unknown art in this era. Even a thousand years ago, ordinary humans could manage only fifth-order sorcery at most. Yet this man—Duke Crystalia—employed the highest levels of magic.

Roooooooooooooar!

Veira let out a savage howl, easily shaking off the gravity well enveloping her. The Dragon Lord's scales had an inherent resistance to sorcery, and even a powerful, eighth-order spell could manage only to stall her. Veira raged, her golden eyes glinting threateningly as she opened her jaws.

"I'll tear your throat out!" she growled.

"Veira, wait. Let me speak to him," Leonis called, then he returned his attention to the strange man. "You wear the form of a human and yet weave the power of a bygone age. Just who are you?"

The sharp, ice-blue eyes examined Leonis as though only noticing him for the first time.

"That's the uniform of a Holy Swordsman. The Seventh Assault Garden. Hmm...," the man muttered. "A minion of the Dragon Lord? Do you wear the form of a child to lull your opponents into a sense of carelessness?"

"..."

Leonis remained silent. It seemed the person resembling Duke Crystalia was yet ignorant of Leonis's true identity.

And there's no reason to relinquish that information.

However, he was familiar with the Seventh Assault Garden, which meant he was definitely a person of this era. Was he truly Riselia's father?

"I know you, Duke Edward Crystalia," Leonis stated.

Beating around the bush was unbecoming of the Undead King. He hoped to strike at the heart of the matter and shake up his adversary, aiming to glean information from his reaction. The man's expression didn't change much, but his keen glare narrowed somewhat.

"So you know me. That is not so unusual. Refugees from outside the city might be unfamiliar with me, but many people know my face."

Leonis nodded. "Yes, I imagine. You are regarded as a hero of humanity, after all. However, the fact you draw breath is not well known, is it?"

Six years ago, Duke Crystalia had died in battle against the Voids. Riselia told Leonis that the rescue unit had failed to recover her father's body. A Stampede left little remaining in its wake, so that wasn't too unusual. However, there was one element that had left Leonis puzzled.

In the ruins of the Third Assault Garden, Leonis had gathered the ghosts of the Crystalia Knights under his command, but Duke Crystalia's spirit had been conspicuously absent. Leonis wasn't the sort to overlook the soul of a great hero. Was this man he now faced truly Duke Crystalia himself, or perhaps...?

"Indeed. I was recorded as a casualty," the man resembling Riselia's father replied indifferently.

"Who are you?" Leonis questioned. "Are you the real Duke Crystalia?"

"That's a question without an answer. *I am he, and at the same time, he is I.*"

"Nonsense," Leonis spat out in annoyance. "If you won't answer, I'll simply force the truth from you."

"Hey, he's my prey!" Veira interjected.

"I see, but unfortunately, I have something to ask of you as well." The man pointed his finger at Leonis. "Dominate, Wheel of Fortune—"

His ring-shaped Holy Sword shone once again.

Slash!

Before Duke Crystalia could manifest his Holy Sword, his arm suddenly flew through the air. A blade of transparent water had cleaved it off.

"...!"

Duke Crystalia whirled around to find a beautiful girl with cold, calm eyes standing atop the raging water. She stood cloaked in a watery raiment, her hair the color of amethyst.

"Rivaiz Deep Sea..." The man regarded her with eyes wide. "So you escaped the fate woven for you by the Wheel of Fortune..."

"Seizing control of my mind is the height of arrogance." She was expressionless, and her tone was hushed, but rage surged in her eyes. Rivaiz extended an arm and declared, "You will pay for that crime with your life."

Bwooooooooooooosh!

A massive cyclone rose from the ocean, loosing a flurry of liquid blades. Veira chanted a spell in dragon tongue, Draconic Light Armor—Griyaslig, conjuring a barrier around herself. They couldn't afford to get caught in the cross fire here. Leonis jumped for cover inside the Dragon Lord's shield.

Duke Crystalia evaded the volley with poise. However, upon seeing the cyclone of water that extended up to the sky destroy part of the Azure Hold, he frowned.

"Challenging two Dark Lords to battle would place me at a disadvantage," he whispered, eyes flitting to his missing right arm for a moment. "I already have what I need."

Crack, crack, crack—

A gigantic fissure centered upon the Azure Hold ran through the air.

What?! Leonis could scarcely believe what he saw.

Cracks in space heralded the arrival of the Voids.

"The Azure Hold! What is this?!" Veira demanded.

"You know nothing of this ruin, Dragon Lord," Duke Crystalia said.

"...What?!"

"This structure is the original template of the human cities. A gate with which to reach the stars."

Crack, crack, crack...

The tear consumed all around it. The leviathan in the water began to vanish into the breach.

"Dark Lords, you cannot escape the fate chosen by my goddess." So saying, the man with Duke Crystalia's countenance disappeared into the spatial rift.

"Goddess... Did he just say goddess?!" Leonis cried.

A memory flashed in his mind, one of the Goddess of Rebellion, Roselia Ishtaris. He knew only one who ever called her "my goddess."

"You...you're...!"

The only Dark Lord who lacked a body of his own, who existed by possessing vessels. A Dark Lord who originated from beyond this dimension and was capable of opening gates to other worlds.

"Azra-Ael, the Devil of the Underworld!"

The moment Leonis intoned the name...

Shatter!

...the world broke apart like fractured glass.

CHAPTER 2

SHARY THE BODY DOUBLE

A boat bobbed along a foggy lake. Riselia sat in the little vessel, clad in a white dress. With her was Leonis, wearing his Excalibur Academy uniform. Birds chirped from somewhere beyond the misty shore.

"E-erm...L-Leo..." Riselia, cheeks flushed, cast an upturned look at the boy sitting opposite her.

"What is it, Miss Selia?" he replied while rowing.

"I, erm...I want a...reward...," Riselia admitted in a bashful yet coaxing tone.

Leonis smiled teasingly. "You're being indecent, Miss Selia. Aren't you a noble's daughter?"

"Ah, er..." The girl's face reddened at the comment.

"Do you want it that badly?" Leonis reached out and twined a silver strand of hair around his finger.

"...Y-yes..."

Leonis's oddly bullyish attitude was a bit different from how he usually acted, and for some reason, it made Riselia's heart beat faster. However, she sensed something a bit off, too.

Did Leo always talk like this...?

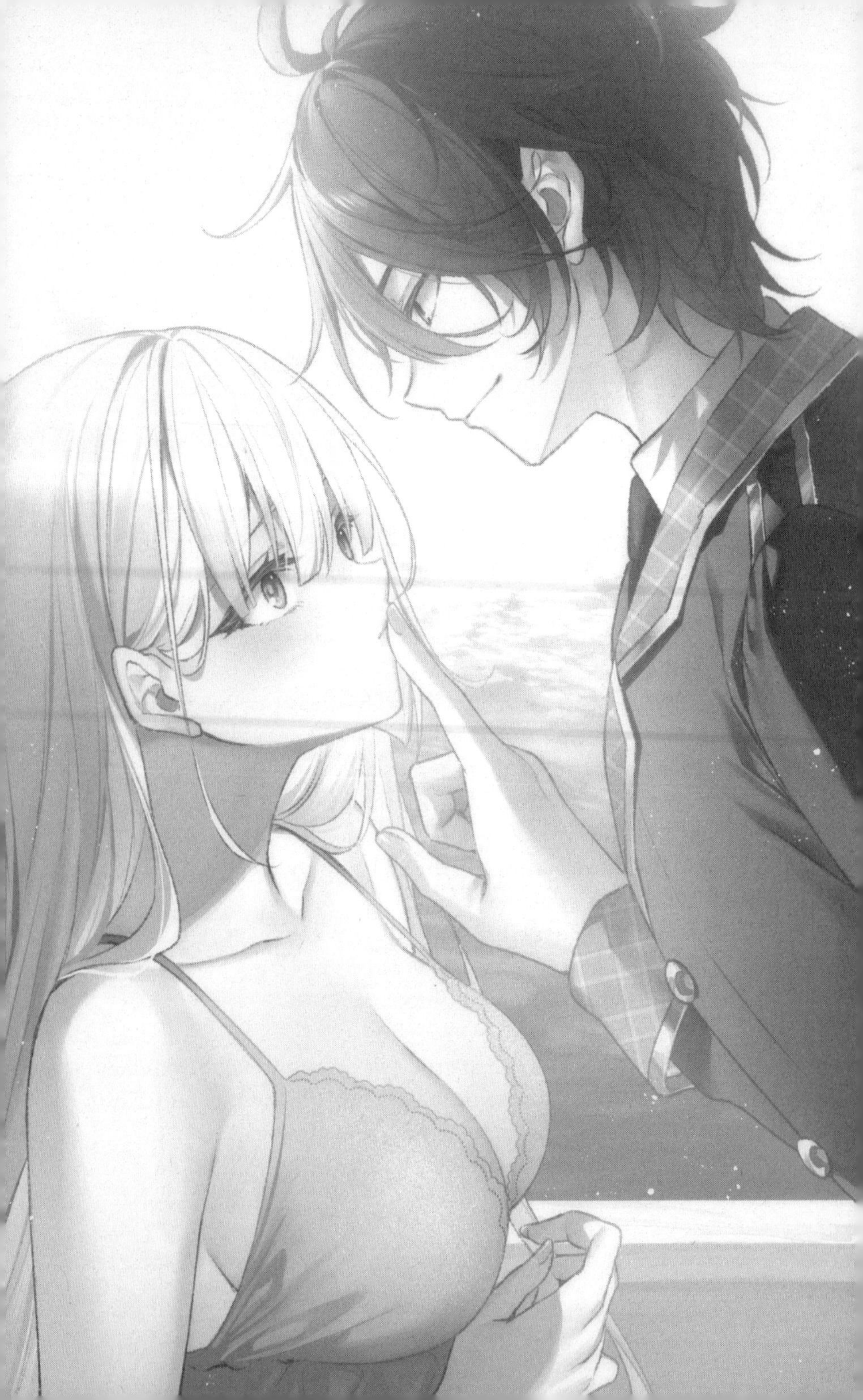

He also appeared taller. It was difficult to tell because they were seated, but he looked to be the same height as Riselia.

Is it because he's a growing boy?

Leonis gently placed his finger on her lips.

"L-Leo..." Riselia's eyes grew blank. She began to lick his fingertip.

"No. You don't have permission yet."

"Huh...?"

"You need to be good and ask for it."

"Leo, please... Don't be mean..." She lapped at the digit touching her lips.

"Heh-heh. What am I going to do with you...? Fine. Go ahead."

She bit down on his finger. Leonis grimaced slightly at the sweet, gentle pain.

"...Mm...Leeeeeo... Mha. ♪"

"H-hey...Miss Selia?"

A single finger just wasn't enough. Caught in a daze, Riselia pushed Leonis down on the shaking boat and sank her fangs into his throat.

"Hee-hee, you're not getting away, Leo. ♪"

"Miss Selia, you're acting strange... Miss Selia, listen to me!" Leonis thrashed, ultimately capsizing the boat.

Bonk!

"O-ow!"

There was a blunt thud. Riselia cradled her head with both hands while groaning in pain.

"G-geez, what are you doing, Leo... Huh?"

Riselia rubbed her bleary eyes, realizing she was wearing pajamas. Morning light broke through the curtains, illuminating her argent locks. Her ice-blue eyes were still half closed.

A pillow rested on her lap, riddled with bite marks, some of which had torn out the stuffing. Riselia sat up and looked around.

She wasn't in a lake surrounded by the woods, nor was there any boat in sight. This was a hotel room, and she was sitting on the floor next to a bed with messy sheets.

"My word. Just what kind of dream were you having?" an exasperated voice criticized her from above.

"...?!"

Riselia looked up, flustered, and saw Leonis glaring down at her coldly.

"Ah, Leo... Good morning."

"Good grief. You're still half asleep." Leonis leaned in, pinching the girl hard on the cheek, which did serve to chase away the drowsiness.

"Ngh, it's not even four in the morning yet!" Riselia protested as she stood to change from her wrinkled pajamas.

"We have morning training. Don your training gear."

"Training?!"

"My lor—I mean, my master ordered me to make you stronger," Leonis stated, bowing his head courteously.

The person Riselia was speaking to wasn't the real Leonis. It was one of his minions acting as his double. It wasn't unusual for Leonis to use imposters to skip lectures at the academy, but in most instances, he sent disguised skeleton soldiers in his stead. This Leonis, however, was someone different.

"But still, four in the morning is too early!"

"Unlike my lor—my master, I have no intention of coddling you. If you ask me, he's sweet with you. Sweeter than sugared doughnuts."

"Doughnuts?" Riselia blinked at this odd choice of analogy.

"Hurry up and get changed."

"...Fiiine."

Riselia had no choice but to obey the false Leonis's oddly strict orders.

◆

As the elevator descended, its window offered a view of the capital's morning scenery. The Shangri-la Resort stood deserted, its liveliness from the prior evening feeling like a lie. Riselia placed a hand on the glass while peering out to sea.

Leo...

He—the real Leonis—had departed last night to help that girl with the flaming hair, his so-called comrade. And though he promised to return as soon as possible, he also said he might not make it to the Holy Sword Dance Festival in time.

You're okay out there, right, Leo?

Riselia was fine with him not returning in time for the festival, but she still worried about his safety. She'd given him the go-ahead—it had been the right thing to do—but that didn't make the worry any easier to manage.

The girl looked away, biting her lip.

From the hotel lobby, the two made their way to the Shangri-la Resort's natural park. Riselia gazed at Leonis's body double's back while walking.

"...What is it?" He suddenly turned around, startling Riselia. "You were staring at me, weren't you?"

"Ah, y-yeah..." Riselia nodded hurriedly. Did he have eyes in the back of his head? "I was just wondering about your name. I'll call you Leo with the others, of course, but what about when it's just the two of us? Should I stick to Leo, or do you have a real name?"

Leonis's replacement gestured pensively. "In truth, I feel that referring to our master by such a nickname is frivolous of you. However, since my lor—I mean, since he allows it, I suppose I shall accept it as well."

"Okay. Let's do our best to get along, Leo. ♪"

Leonis furrowed his brow in displeasure.

"That aside, I'd still like to know your real name," Riselia added.

"Why? My real name is of no consequence."

Riselia wouldn't be deterred. "That's not true. You're different from the bone soldiers Leo summons all the time...right?"

"...I am not a skeleton, no," Leonis answered, looking offended by the implication.

"Right. That's good. If there were any more skellies around, I wouldn't be able to tell you apart."

Leonis often summoned undead to help with Riselia's training, but since they were all jumbled-up bones, she couldn't tell which was which. It was very confusing.

Leonis stopped in his tracks and pulled a face. "You can't tell skeleton soldiers apart?"

"No, well, sometimes I can...," Riselia said, holding up an index finger. "The strongest ones are Amilas, Dorug, and Nefisgal. And the one that's kind of yellow is the sniper, Zolua. The one with the big crack is the Death Swordfighter Feiden, and the one with the twisted arm is Grayfauzer. The one with the dented skeleton is the Dark Priest Meridore, and the lady skeleton is—"

"W-wait, hold on just a minute!" Leonis interjected. "You really remember the names and characteristics of all the skeletons?"

"Of course. They're my teachers, after all." Riselia nodded, as if to confirm that much was obvious.

"..." Leonis was stunned.

"I'll remember your name, too, so tell me."

"...I-I'm not telling."

"Oh, come on, it totally felt like you were going to!"

"If, and only if, the day comes when I acknowledge your worth, I will tell you my name."

Leonis—actually Shary—then mumbled that such a time would

never arrive, and she averted her gaze. Upon reaching the entrance to the natural park, she immediately ordered, "Five laps around the park."

"What, that's all?" Riselia asked, disappointed.

The park's outer circumference was two kilorels in length. It wasn't much of a distance. Even Excalibur Academy's basic training was more severe, and Riselia had an undead body.

"You will have to wear this, though." Shary snapped her fingers, and the shadow at Riselia's feet began to writhe.

"Wh-what?!" Riselia cried as darkness crept up her body, binding her legs and hands. "I-it's...heavy..."

"I turned your own shadow into weights to restrict you."

"...Weights?" When Riselia looked down, she recognized that her shadow had thinned slightly.

A moment later, the darkness fettering her limbs turned transparent, blending in with her skin. "You will spend the time leading up to the Holy Sword Dance Festival bound as you are now," Shary stated.

"Huh?! B-but, I can't run properly like this!"

"If you put your vampire mana to good use, you will get used to it before long."

"Get used to it... But what about when I sleep, or take a bath?"

"You will tend to your daily needs with them on, of course."

"No way..."

"Riselia Crystalia, I was ordered to train you as my lor—the master's proxy. I am simply abiding by that command." Leonis produced a shadow whip in his hand.

"A whip?" Riselia had a bad feeling about this.

"Now, hurry up and get to running!"

Crack!

"O-okay!" Riselia bolted off, spurred by the sharp noise of the whip against the ground.

◆

A wooden sword cut through the air, whistling. Sakuya stood in the park by the hotel. Swinging practice was part of her daily routine. When she trained in the woods behind the Hræsvelgr dorm, she manifested her Holy Sword, Raikirimaru, but using Holy Swords outside Excalibur Academy premises was strictly forbidden.

Sakuya didn't normally care much for these rules, but Elfiné was the one who'd set the eighteenth platoon up with a private hotel floor, and Sakuya didn't want to cause trouble for her.

I shouldn't drag her name through the mud.

She brought her wooden sword down again, then stopped. Her eyes peered ahead while she pictured a girl who shared her facial features.

Setsura...

Sakuya's older sister was thought to have died nine years ago during the Sakura Orchid's destruction, yet she was alive. She'd returned from the dead...and tried to claim Sakuya's—her younger sister's—life.

She wasn't a fake. There's no doubting it—that was really Setsura.

The image of Setsura's cold, sagacious eyes had been burned into Sakuya's mind. Setsura had released the Sakura Orchid guardian deity sealed within the Seventh Assault Garden's Mana Furnace and summoned the very Void Lord who'd destroyed her homeland.

Why had she returned from the dead? What did she seek to achieve...?

Sakuya returned her attention to the top of her wooden sword. Training was about more than the Holy Sword Dance Festival, which was only days away. She was bound to lock blades with her sister again.

I can't beat her. Not yet.

Cold sweat ran down Sakuya's neck. Despite all attempts, she couldn't envision defeating her older sister. Her left eye throbbed painfully from behind its eye patch.

The mystic eye of time, granted to her by the man who called himself a Dark Lord. Sakuya couldn't take off the eye patch yet. If she did, the mystic eye's power would start eating away at her.

I can't beat Setsura without mastering the power of this gift...

Sakuya relaxed her muscles and leaned the wooden sword against a tree. No sooner had she done so, however, than a sound from the bushes set her on edge.

"...?"

Sakuya turned and saw a large black hound emerge from the bushes.

"Oh, Fluffymaru. Want some snacks?"

Fluffymaru hesitated for only a moment, barking in reply. Sakuya offered a roasted rice cracker from her sleeve, which the dog accepted gladly. Sakuya smiled and scratched Fluffymaru's head.

"Heh-heh, you're as fluffy as ever, Fluffymaru."

"Woof..."

"Do you like it here? You're just like the first Fluffymaru the Black."

The original Fluffymaru the Black was a combat hound raised by the Sakura Orchid royal family to guard the princess priestesses. Sakuya and Setsura cherished Fluffymaru the Black when they were young, but the animal perished with so many others on that awful day nine years ago. Sakuya scratched and patted the dog, seeing her old one's likeness in him.

"Mm. Is that Miss Selia...?" Sakuya wondered aloud after spotting a silver-haired young woman desperately circumnavigating the park. "Early morning training, huh? Quite admirable..."

◆

"Lady Selia, what's wrong?!"

Regina's eyes were wide in shock when Riselia returned to the hotel. Despite appearing like a secluded noble lady, Riselia subjected herself to rigorous exercise. As a result, her stamina exceeded that of most other academy students.

Yet now Riselia was...wholly worn out. She'd collapsed upon the table after dragging herself to the meeting room. It was quite unusual to see a dignified duke's daughter act so improperly.

"A-are you all right? Have some water." Regina offered a glass and patted her mistress on the back.

"Y-yes, I'm fine. I'm just a little...tired...from my early morning training, is all..."

"You were out exercising this early?" Regina frowned. "But we're going to be training after this, too."

"...Yeah. It's just, Leo—"

"Good morning, Miss Regina," the boy greeted her as he entered the room.

"Ah, good morning, kid, ♪" Regina answered. Leaning close to him, she whispered, "Say, kid. Lady Selia's acting all weird. Did you do something to her?"

Leonis looked away awkwardly. "E-erm. I might have been a bit harsh when I trained her."

After a short while, Elfiné and Sakuya arrived, and the morning meeting commenced. Holding a discussion during breakfast was the eighteenth platoon's tradition. Its members had partaken of the hotel restaurant's buffet on their first day here, but this time, Regina had prepared a meal in the common room kitchen using ingredients purchased from the city.

She'd made her own special pizza recipe with tomato slices, onions, large pieces of ham, and melted cheese, all baked to a crisp in the oven. To go with it, she'd also prepared white fish soup, salad with roasted walnuts, and yogurt with homemade plum jam she'd brought from the Hræsvelgr dorm.

"Ahh...Miss Regina, can I have some more?" Leonis asked with glittering eyes after stuffing his cheeks with Regina's pizza.

"Eat up. ♪ Wow, you've got a healthy appetite today, kid."

"...I—I do?"

Elfiné giggled and smiled at him. "Maybe you've hit a growth spurt. Here, have some coffee."

"Thank you." Leonis accepted the mug and sipped its contents. *"Pfff! Cough, cough!"*

Leonis choked on his coffee.

"...I-it's bitter!" he exclaimed.

"But we put in lots of sugar, as always."

"Huh? Ah, y-yeah, you did..."

Leonis nodded evasively, shoveling yogurt into his mouth to cleanse his palate.

I guess filling in for the real thing is a bit difficult... Riselia watched the imposter, feeling a bit nervous.

Once everyone was settled, the platoon began their meeting.

"This year's Holy Sword Dance Festival will be held on the Eighth Assault Garden, which is still under construction," Elfiné said, displaying an image on her terminal's monitor.

The Eighth Assault Garden, Nebulous, was a new city under construction at the capital. It was roughly 78 percent complete, and was coupled to the industrial area's new Float VII.

Once complete, Nebulous would be part of the Assault Garden Strike Force, led by the Seventh Assault Garden. It would engage in large-scale Void eradication missions.

"It may have been chosen as the event site to serve as a demonstration for immigrating citizens," Elfiné speculated, tapping on the terminal.

"I suppose it'll be a lot like the urban combat training the senior students have in their curriculums," Riselia commented.

Excalibur Academy's urban combat training used real city environments in the Seventh Assault Garden. Elfiné was the only senior in the eighteenth platoon and thus the only one in the group privy to this training. However, all the girls had experience with urban warfare from the previous Stampedes.

Elfiné nodded. "The rules will be based on the typical urban training team bouts. Finding core flags placed around the area will be the best way to get points. Of course, just like in ordinary matches, destroying an opponent's Holy Sword or knocking them out of commission helps our score, too."

"What about our initial positioning?" Sakuya inquired.

"We don't have to worry about protecting a base this time. Each unit will be deployed to one of the Eighth Assault Garden's areas randomly and will need to gather information while collecting core flags. Regardless of our initial position, we won't know where the other squads are."

"Well, our platoon has the edge when it comes to intelligence, thanks to your Holy Sword, Miss Finé."

"True. But other groups have scanner-type Holy Swords, too."

Elfiné called up data about the other platoons' representatives on her terminal. Humanity had established six facilities that trained Holy Swordsmen, including Excalibur Academy. The Capital's Elysion Academy, the Fifth Assault Garden's Anti-Void Research Institute, the Fourth Assault Garden's Academia, the Second Assault Garden's Military Instruction School, and the Human Church's St. Eluminas Monastery.

Elfiné's data included information on each school's representatives, but it consisted only of public information. There'd be no way of knowing how strong the representatives were until seeing them in action.

For example, Riselia had only recently awakened to her Holy Sword, and Leonis was a newcomer, so most others didn't have a grasp of their abilities. In all likelihood, other participants were wariest of Sakuya, who'd held the record for slaying large Voids since she was a young girl.

"Lady Chatres is as overwhelming as ever," Riselia whispered while looking at the terminal screen.

Chatres Ray O'ltriese, one of Elysion Academy's representatives. The third princess of the empire was considered the strongest Holy Swordswoman among all students. Her abilities went beyond her powers; she was also a skilled commander and highly trusted by her platoon.

"We're not going to lose. Let's do this!" Riselia said, despite the many formidable opponents.

Everyone in the room nodded.

◆

The Central Garden—the capital. Located at its core was the very symbol of the Human Integrated Empire, the palace. This brickwork fortress, built in the style of the old kingdoms, gave the impression that it had gone untouched by the magitech revolution.

Since it was essentially a garrison, it was surrounded by a vast forest and gardens. The palace alone covered an area roughly half that of Excalibur Academy. Gardens within the woods surrounding the structure were open to the public.

His villa was nestled within the palace's premises.

"Oh my. I wasn't expecting guests today."

The man, who was tending to a decorative plant, faced the door, sensing that someone had arrived.

"I'm surprised you noticed me, Your Highness."

A half-transparent woman materialized before the closed door. She was clad in a researcher's lab coat and had beautiful black hair.

This woman, a senior research officer for the Phillet Company, had an espionage-type Holy Sword that allowed her to reduce her presence to nothing.

"Ah, it's you, Clauvia. I suppose I can't scold the guards for letting someone get past them, then."

The emperor's younger brother and second in the line of succession—Alexios Ray O'ltriese—greeted his unexpected guest casually. The man in his midthirties possessed delicate features. He was tall, slender, and appeared quite unreliable, despite being the younger sibling of the most powerful person in the empire.

"I have a report regarding *that* matter, Your Highness," Clauvia whispered.

Alexios's face suddenly became quite serious.

"...Did you find something?"

"It's observation data from Alexandria's research institute. An unidentified gigantic mass was detected moving at high speeds over the ocean twenty-five hundred kilorels to the south. The institute presumes it's a gigantic Void, but the details are inconclusive. It seemed to be en route to the capital for a while, but the observation tools lost sight of it halfway through. It's believed to have moved out of the region where it was first detected."

"Hmm. You think it was a Dark Lord?"

"In all likelihood..." Clauvia nodded. "Its gigantic mass and how it moved across the sea means it's probably the Dark Lord that reigned over the ocean."

"Yes. The one said to rule the ancient world's seas, the destroyer of twelve oceanic kingdoms. So another Dark Lord has appeared. Perhaps it was roused by tectonic movements on the seabed. Then again, someone may have purposefully awoken it."

"We don't know. At the very least, we believe its activity isn't connected to the Voids, unlike the one we discovered in the tundra."

"That's a stroke of luck. Losing our trump card, the Dragon

Lord, was a painful blow…" Alexios shrugged and stroked the decorative plant's leaves. "It seems the prophecy Duke Edward Crystalia left behind was true after all. The Dark Lords, the life-forms that dominated the world a thousand years ago, are returning."

The Dark Lords were fiction reserved for fairy tales. Duke Crystalia, Alexios's sworn friend, had spent his life pursuing evidence of the Dark Lords' existence. He'd proposed wielding their destructive power to defeat the Voids. Over time, this came to be known as the Dark Lord Project.

For all their power, the Dark Lords were enemies of humanity, and the method of controlling them was still in the early stages. Most of the supposed eight Dark Lords yet remained a mystery, too.

One thing was certain, though: the immensely powerful Dark Lords did exist.

"The Dragon Lord, the Lord of the Seas. Then the next one to rise should be the Undead King."

The Undead King was the most feared of the Dark Lords, so much so that ancient peoples were scared to speak of him. This was stated in Duke Crystalia's posthumous manuscripts. It was said that the Undead King blighted the earth and employed the dead, resurrecting the departed in blasphemous forms.

Raising the dead. Was anyone, Dark Lord or not, genuinely capable of that? Either way…

"It's ironic. The Dark Lords might become our kind's greatest hope…," Alexios whispered, gazing into the distance.

❖

The empire's third princess, Chatres Ray O'ltriese, suddenly stopped in her tracks. She'd been wandering the palace gardens. Her eyes took on a dangerous glint, and she raised her fair eyebrows. She'd just spotted a woman walk out of her uncle's mansion.

That Phillet vixen is trying to curry favor with Uncle Alexios again, is she...?

Rumors whispered that this woman, Clauvia Phillet, was her uncle's lover. And Chatres believed them.

How unsightly. And Uncle Alexios is no better...

This fastidious young woman, driven by a pure sense of justice, couldn't bear to see this.

"Did something happen, Chatres?" a lovely voice asked her, concerned.

"Oh, my apologies, Altiria. It's nothing." Chatres turned around, donning a gentle smile.

Altiria was pinching the sleeve of Chatres's uniform and looking up at her older sister. Her hair shone like gold, and her eyes were green like her sibling's. Altiria Ray O'ltriese was the empire's fourth princess.

"...Really? You looked a bit scary..."

My little sister is a shrewd, observant one, isn't she?

Impressed by Altiria's intuition, Chatres took a moment to compose herself better. Whenever she interacted with Altiria, she had to play the ideal older sister. She couldn't show her displeasure at the presence of their uncle's lover. There were other reasons for her foul mood, however.

Reporters had disturbed the siblings' long overdue lunch date earlier. With the Holy Sword Dance Festival right around the corner, the media was dying to wring an interview out of Chatres, last year's champion.

At first, Chatres responded to the inquiries politely, believing that was her duty as the winner. But reporters had pressed their advantage over the last few days, asking more intimate questions. It was intolerable. And while Chatres wanted nothing more than to blow them away with her Holy Sword, she had to maintain appearances as a princess of the empire.

Chatres knew this, of course. She was widely regarded as the best on her team and the strongest Holy Swordswoman among all the students. There was no denying that her beauty stood well above the norm as well. For someone like that to command so much attention was to be expected.

However, she could not help but take offense at how reporters pestered her for comments on Riselia Crystalia's participation in this year's Holy Sword Dance Festival. She was the daughter of Duke Crystalia, a hero, and was one of the few survivors of the Third Assault Garden's destruction. Those qualities and her unusual awakening to the power of her Holy Sword set her apart. She was the kind of idol the media lapped up. However, Chatres had little interest in the girl.

She bore no ill will for Riselia Crystalia. Still, she did feel that a special entry brought in solely to drum up attention could only amount to so much... Ultimately, Chatres decided that she would turn down any new requests for interviews.

Time spent with my younger sister is far too precious to be wasted on such frivolities.

She placed a hand on Altiria's head.

...Maybe I dote on her too much. Yet who could blame me, with her being so sweet?

Watching Altiria grin reminded Chatres that she supposedly had another younger sister. The princess had learned of this only a few years ago. This other sibling was treated as having never existed under an agreement between the royal family and the Human Church. Soon after her birth, she was handed over to some noble who adopted and raised her.

She must be fifteen by now.

Despite being her older sister, Chatres had been powerless to help that unknown girl. Of course, Chatres was a child at the time, but she still regretted allowing it to happen.

I can only hope she knew a happy life...

"Chatres...stop, you're treating me like a child."

"...Oh. My apologies." Chatres gave an apologetic smile and took her hand off Altiria's head. "I should be going. My subordinates are waiting..."

"Oh, okay!"

The two of them walked through the garden together.

"I look forward to seeing you perform at the festival," Altiria remarked.

Chatres nodded, brimming with confidence. "Yes, you should watch from the best seat available. My Holy Sword will reign supreme."

Altiria suddenly hung her head awkwardly. "Oh, e-erm..."

"What's wrong?" Chatres inquired.

"I was just wondering, Chatres... Will you be fighting Sir Leonis?" Altiria asked sheepishly.

"Leonis?"

Seeing her sister fidget bashfully, Chatres recalled the ten-year-old boy from Riselia Crystalia's platoon. Apparently, he'd been on the *Hyperion* during the hijacking incident. Altiria seemed to be under the mistaken impression that he was the one who'd saved her.

Chatres didn't have the heart to tell her younger sister that she'd gotten the wrong idea about how events played out.

"Don't worry. I won't fight seriously against a child," Chatres assured her nonchalantly, shrugging in an attempt to soothe her sibling's concerns.

"If I may, Chatres, let me warn you: Sir Leonis is very strong."

"Yes, right. I'll make sure to be wary."

The strongest student Holy Swordswoman watched Altiria pout and puff up her cheeks, noting that even that was adorable when it came from her little sister.

CHAPTER 3

THROWN TO ANOTHER WORLD

"...?"

When Leonis opened his eyes, he saw a vast, windswept wilderness. A cloud of black dust covered his field of vision like a swarm of insects.

Where...am I?

After blinking a few times, Leonis tried to look around. Countless odd rock formations dotted the wastes, but he couldn't make out anything else of note. This barren land extended as far as the eye could see. The sky was red as blood and unmarred by any clouds.

The gigantic leviathan was gone.

"...It seems I've wandered into some kind of other realm, an underworld perhaps."

After a moment's confusion at the unusual sight, Leonis concluded that the Azure Hold had been transported to another dimension or world, and he'd been caught in that process.

I never knew that aerial fortress could traverse the planes.

It was just like *his* bastion—the Otherworldly Castle.

Was that really Azra-Ael? Leonis wondered, placing a hand on his chin.

Azra-Ael—a visitor from a different dimension. Roselia Ishtaris had summoned the Devil of the Underworld from some other realm. Of the eight Dark Lords, he was the most shrouded in mystery... None save the goddess herself saw their true form.

Azra-Ael was believed to lack a physical body. Only by possessing a vessel were they able to use their powers.

Why, then, had they taken over Duke Crystalia, Riselia's father...?

No... Him being possessed by Azra-Ael is still only a theory.

Still, he could freely traverse dimensional gates, wielded lost sorcery, and knew of the Dark Lords. And most suspicious of all...

He said, "my goddess."

Of all the Dark Lords, the only ones to swear genuine fealty to Roselia Ishtaris were Leonis and Azra-Ael. The others all used the Dark Lords' Armies as a means to further their own ambitions.

The Devil of the Underworld always respectfully referred to Roselia as "my goddess." However, there was no knowing for certain if Duke Crystalia had been referring to Roselia when he used the phrase.

"...I suppose he flew off somewhere."

Leonis couldn't see the man anywhere, and the Azure Hold and that leviathan were absent as well. Veira had vanished, too, as had...

Rivaiz, eh...?

Rivaiz Deep Sea, one half of the Lord of the Seas, was a sea sprite. Somehow, she'd broken free from the man's mind-controlling Holy Sword.

Before worrying about anything else, I need to figure out how to escape this world...

Leonis marched through the sandstorm-buffeted wastes. He already knew of one way to return home. It wasn't a field he was exceptionally proficient in, but as a master of all manners of sorcery, he knew multiple spells to create gates to other dimensions. In fact, the underground that the Demon Wolf Pack used as their hideout had been created with one. It linked the Seventh Assault Garden to a different plane.

Opening portals to other dimensions was no simple feat, though. One needed to have the coordinates of their prior world, or else there was no telling where the magic would send them. It might fling them to the bottom of the sea or inside a boulder.

When Leonis was at his full might as the Undead King, he might have braved the risks and tried it anyway, but his current body was that of a fragile ten-year-old boy. He couldn't take such a gamble.

I suppose my only recourse is to seek out Azra-Ael.

Leonis didn't know how large this world was, but if Azra-Ael was moving with the Azure Hold, finding them wouldn't be too challenging.

Suddenly, a massive shadow passed over the land. Leonis looked up.

"...What's that?!"

A large creature resembling a stingray glided through the air. Had to measure over a hundred meltes end to end. Its gigantic fins undulated with every movement, scattering a nauseating miasma as it lorded over the sky. Countless arms sprouted out of its torso, each writhing seemingly of its own will.

Two large, white fangs extended from its mouth... No, they weren't fangs. Careful inspection revealed that its maw was filled with Voids. The being's appearance was an affront to life itself, and even Leonis, the Undead King, felt only disgust and aversion to it.

"...A Void?" he whispered.

Immediately, the flying monster changed bearing and looked directly at him.

It spotted me from that high up?!

The hands sticking out from its stomach started glowing, each of them alight with a different elemental affinity. It was the radiance of sorcery.

"Tch...!"

Boom, boom, boom, boom!

A shower of offensive spells bombarded the rocky wasteland. Intense flames erupted, blowing away the dust. And at the epicenter of the explosion...

"...So these despicable Void monsters run rampant in this world, too," Leonis muttered while the black smoke cleared.

He'd cast a defensive spell, so there wasn't so much as a speck of soot on his Excalibur Academy uniform. After retrieving the Staff of Sealed Sins from his shadow, Leonis held it high, chanting another spell.

"I'll reduce you to ashes—eighth-order flame spell—Al Gu Belzelga!"

Boooom!

A fireball erupted from the rod, striking its mark directly. It bore a hole in the gigantic Void's stomach, from which Void miasma gushed out like blood.

"Oh, you can withstand the strongest of fire spells? Quite the durable one, aren't you?"

A moment before the spell hit the Void, the hands sprouting from its stomach all deployed defensive spells as one. However, most of those arms had been destroyed by Leonis's magic anyway, and the Void's regeneration couldn't keep up.

"■■■■■■■■■■■■!"

The Void let out a furious howl and opened its mouth.

I see. It's like a host for Void parasites.

The swarm that emerged from the gigantic Void droned like insects and flew at Leonis. He shrugged and tapped the Staff of Sealed Sins against the ground.

"Very well. I am a bit tired from repeated fighting, but I'll play along for now." Cackling wickedly, he intoned a new spell.

Before he could finish, however...

Shatter!

...a sound like shattering glass rent the air.

"—What?!"

A blade of water laced with mana sped across the wasteland, cutting through the swarm of Voids like a hot knife through butter. It continued farther, cleaving into the gigantic Void overhead.

Miasma spurted across the red sky. The 100-melte-long Void was then cut into four cubes, then eight, then sixteen, all of which fell to the ground with heavy thuds. Leonis hurried to evade the tumbling blocks of flesh, searching for the source of the water blade.

Standing atop a misshaped rock formation stood an expressionless girl, her hair the color of amethyst.

"...Rivaiz Deep Sea," Leonis whispered, although she didn't hear him.

The girl watched him, gaze as deep as the ocean floor. "Human child. Who are you, really?"

Her question echoed softly through the wasteland covered in Void corpses.

◆

"Hmm. I never imagined that the Undead King would adopt such an adorable form." Rivaiz patted Leonis on the head a few times.

"Grr... Don't touch me, Lord of the Seas!" Leonis brushed her hand away, his hair standing on end.

The Lord of the Seas had been hesitant to believe Leonis's claim that he was the Undead King. When he showed her the Staff of Sealed Sins, the Dark Lords' Armies' symbol of death, and summoned his prided legion of skeleton soldiers, she accepted the story immediately.

According to Rivaiz, many sorcerers used undead fighters, but the only one who could maintain a contingent of splendidly polished bone warriors was the Undead King.

Yes, that's right, that's exactly right. Leonis nodded to himself, satisfied.

He was always quite picky when it came to choosing his skeletons. Leonis gave a dry cough and looked up at Rivaiz.

"Lord of the Seas, there's something I wish to ask you."

The girl nodded arrogantly. "You have permission to inquire, Undead King."

Condescending, aren't you? Leonis thought, blind to his own shortcomings. Needless to say, the Dark Lords were all quite arrogant.

"Were you under that human's mind control?" Leonis questioned.

At this, Rivaiz's eyes glinted ominously. "Yes. My pride as the Lord of the Seas has been tarnished by ever allowing it to occur." Perhaps recalling what happened angered her, because her water mantle started writhing, alive with mana.

"I'd always believed you were beset upon by the Spellweaver of the Six Heroes and the battle ended in mutual destruction," Leonis remarked.

"Indeed. The leviathan and I defeated Diruda the Spellweaver just as he bested us, and we sank to the depths along with the Underwater Stronghold."

"So you mean you were not completely slain," Leonis said.

Rivaiz bobbed her head. "However, Diruda's powerful magic drove me to the brink. Thus, I decided to change to a jewel that would slowly absorb mana from the ocean floor until the day came for me to rise again."

A thousand years passed while she slumbered.

"At some point, that human found the jewel at the bottom of the sea and released me... I cannot remember precisely when it happened. But it was not too long ago." Rivaiz bit her lip gently. "Having been rudely awakened from my peaceful slumber, I tried to tear the scoundrel to bits. But the human anticipated as much and had a trump card to hold me in check."

Leonis raised an eyebrow. "A trump card?"

"The cur had already dominated my other half—the leviathan," Rivaiz replied bitterly.

"You mean you weren't the one to resurrect the leviathan?"

"No. I don't know what heretical means that human employed to restore my other half, but he succeeded. Spurred by wrath over the theft of my kindred spirit, I challenged him to battle and was defeated."

Rivaiz Deep Sea, the Lord of the Seas, was seen as the strongest of all the Dark Lords. However, the position was held by two beings that acted as one Dark Lord. Rivaiz, the Sea Sprite Queen, and the single greatest form of life, the leviathan. Only when the two acted as one did they function as the Lord of the Seas.

And with the leviathan taken from her, Rivaiz had no chance of winning.

"And so I succumbed to his mental domination," Rivaiz explained, her voice trembling with anger.

"Do you remember what happened while you were under his thrall?" Leonis questioned.

"Mm. I vaguely recall what occurred slightly before I was freed from his control. I remember fighting you..." Rivaiz leaned forward and gazed into Leonis's eyes. "Undead King. In defeating me, you have freed me from that man's domination. I owe you a debt of gratitude."

"...I see," Leonis replied vaguely.

He wasn't sure if Rivaiz's liberation resulted from his efforts.

It was possible, yet there could have been other factors at play. Perhaps when the man tried to use his Holy Sword on Veira, its hold on Rivaiz waned temporarily. Or...

Leonis's Holy Sword—the Excalibur XX. Maybe it affected other Holy Swords in some way.

Regardless, Rivaiz was only one of his unwitting pawns.

Azra-Ael, the Demon of the Underworld. What did they hope to achieve by awakening a Dark Lord...?

"Incidentally, Undead King...," Rivaiz called out to Leonis, stirring him from contemplation.

"What is it?"

"Where are we?" Rivaiz asked, looking around with a frown.

"Another world," Leonis answered. "Another dimension."

"Another world or dimension?"

"It seems that when the Azure Hold traveled to a different realm, we were transported along with it."

"I see. Yes, the ocean is nowhere to be found."

"It took you this long to notice?" Leonis shrugged in exasperation.

Rivaiz scanned over the blocks of flesh scattered around them.

"What was that unsightly monster earlier? I've never seen a creature of the sort before."

"A Void. Unknown life-forms born of the emptiness."

"Hmm..." Rivaiz cocked her head to one side, seemingly confused.

The gigantic Void's remains still spewed miasma.

I didn't expect to find Voids running rampant in another world.

Maybe this desolate scenery resulted from the destruction the monstrous things sowed.

"I'll be going after that man," Leonis declared, his eyes fixed on the red sky. "I have much to ask him."

"I shall accompany you, then," Rivaiz decided. "I must reclaim my leviathan."

"..."

Leonis took a moment to consider. Although she was in an incomplete state, Rivaiz was still half of a Dark Lord. Her strength was remarkable. And they had fought side by side once a thousand years ago to defeat the God of the Sea. Although Leonis had no way of telling what Rivaiz was thinking, she was still a Dark Lord who was comparatively easy to cooperate with.

"...Very well. Come with me, then." Leonis tapped the Staff of Sealed Sins against the ground. "Come forth, skull dragon!"

Vrrrrrrr...!

A skeletal dragon emerged from the boy's shadow and spread its wings. Leonis sat upon the skull dragon's neck, and Rivaiz hopped atop it softly with the lightness of a flower petal to join him.

"You can fly on your own, can't you?" Leonis asked.

"I merely thought that riding atop the famed Undead King's skull dragon might make for an interesting experience," Rivaiz reasoned coolly.

Leonis shrugged. "It's not my problem if you fall off."

The skull dragon let out an eldritch howl and took to the air.

"Heeeeeeeeey! Stop right there, Leo!"

"...Nn?" Leonis turned around at the familiar voice.

A beautiful girl flew behind the soaring Skull Dragon, her flaming red hair trailing after her.

"Oh. So you were close by, too."

"Don't you 'oh' me! That flashy show you two put on was easy to spot, and I flew over," Veira said, landing with a tap on the skull dragon's snout. "You're going after that man, right?"

"Yes."

"Then I'm coming along. I need to reclaim the Azure Hold from him."

Leonis sighed. "Do as you please."

They were all going in the same direction anyway. Veira eyed Rivaiz, who'd taken her seat on the skull dragon's back.

"Rivaiz, we still have a score to settle over the Azure Hold."

"I have no desire to battle you right now, Dragon Lord." The Lord of the Seas glared back at Veira. "However, if you insist on fighting, I will gladly oblige."

"Hmph. Defeating you when you're without your leviathan would mar my reputation as the Dragon Lord. I'm willing to consider this a cease-fire for now." Veira combed through her crimson hair with one hand.

"Hmph. Very well," Rivaiz accepted.

...Stop picking fights while you're on my skull dragon, you two. Leonis shuddered at the very notion.

"So which way are we flying, Leo?" Veira inquired.

"I don't know," he answered frankly, his eyes fixed forward. "For now, let's see how far this other world goes."

CHAPTER 4

APOSTLES OF THE GODDESS

"—You're still looking with your eyes. There's no point unless you sense them with mana."

"O-okay!" Riselia replied energetically under the blazing sun.

She and the others were at a large, anti-Void weapons training facility, part of the Shangri-la Resort and thus owned by the Phillet Corporation.

The exercise was quite simple. Leonis unleashed mana spheres, and Riselia had to dodge them. At first, she could keep up, but evading became more challenging as the number of orbs increased. While she escaped direct hits, she quickly grew exhausted.

"Haah, haah, haah...," Riselia panted.

"Is this as far as you can go? If this kind of training is enough to make you throw in the towel—"

"...N-not yet! Give me more, please!" Riselia called out, wiping the sweat off her jaw.

"Well, you've got the right attitude, if nothing else. This time, I think I'll get serious."

"Huhhhhhh?!"

It was only then that Riselia understood. *Leo's been holding back this whole time!*

"Go, go, Lady Selia! Keep it up, Lady Selia!" a voice encouraged from nearby.

Riselia turned around, only to find...

"R-Regina?! What are you doing?!"

"I'm cheering you on, Lady Selia! ♪ Go, go, Lady Selia! ♪"

Regina jumped around energetically with pompoms in her hands. For some reason, she'd changed into a cheerleader outfit and appeared to be enjoying it thoroughly.

"S-stop it, this is embarrassing...!" Riselia chided her.

"If anything, I'm the one who should be embarrassed...," Regina replied.

"Then apologize and stop it!"

"Turning your back, are you? Let's add some more balls, then," Leonis said, producing countless mana spheres that sped at Riselia.

Sometime later...

"Here, Lady Selia. A drink."

"Thank you, Regina."

...Riselia, lying faceup on the ground, accepted a sports drink from Regina and gulped it down.

Leonis shrugged. "That should do for morning training."

"M-morning training...?"

"That was just a warm-up. Our session later will be even more demanding," Leonis stated mercilessly.

"Huh...?" Riselia whimpered. "Real Leo, please come back already..."

It was quite unusual to hear Riselia whine aloud.

"Kid, I want to rest a bit. I'm exhausted from all this cheering," Regina said.

"Very well. Use this break to rest up."

Immediately, Riselia sat up. "Why are you so soft on Regina?!"

For some odd reason, this fake Leonis seemed to hold Regina in high regard.

"We'll be meeting up with Miss Finé and Sakuya during the afternoon, right?" Regina asked.

"Yes, that was the plan, but..."

Sakuya had turned down the offer to train together, claiming she needed to do some independent practice. Her methods were unique, so that made sense. Typically, she spent her mornings in the woods behind the Hræsvelgr dorm, cutting falling leaves before they hit the ground or jumping between the trees.

Normal training probably doesn't cut it for her.

◆

Camelot's Area VI—the undeveloped sector. It was originally a generic expansion module for construction of the Third Assault Garden's industrial production plants. However, the Third Assault Garden's destruction six years ago had put that project on hold.

At present, it was used only as a dumping site for construction material. The Linear Rail ran to it to transport supplies. People hardly ever went out there.

Area VI appeared deserted, save for several Artificial Elementals made by the Phillet Company, which patrolled the area.

However, that was only on the surface. Deep below the undeveloped section was an entire underground world. Area VI's bowels served as a home for smugglers, criminals, hooligans, anti-royalty terrorists, and even heretical sects that worshipped the Voids.

"Why doesn't the empire's army crush all these underground organizations?" a girl wondered as she walked down a tunnel illuminated by mana lamps.

Her name was Arle Kirlesio, an elf warrior with beautiful,

pointed ears and jade hair tied in a ponytail. Outwardly, she looked pretty young, but she was, in fact, a seasoned hero. And through some twist of fate that even she couldn't explain adequately, she'd become part of a criminal organization.

Sakuya, who walked beside Arle, replied, "It could stomp them all out together, but it would mean suffering losses. Plus, having them far from the capital's center and gathered in one place makes them easier to handle. The army has quashed a few criminal sects before, but it only made them break into more extreme factions and spread to other Assault Gardens."

"...I see."

Arle recalled that the group she'd fallen in with, the Demon Wolf Pack, was originally an anti-royal terrorist organization.

"Looks like that's the place." Sakuya looked up from her map and pointed ahead.

An intense neon mana glow shone at the far end of the tunnel.

"Are we really going to charge in?" Arle asked.

"Yes. No offense to my upperclassmen, but normal training isn't enough for me. I'm more suited to learning through live combat."

"Er...I see. But why did I have to come along, too?" Arle eyed the other girl, pouting.

This was the first time Sakuya had contacted Arle via her terminal. The elf hero still wasn't sure why.

"I figured I'd get lost on my own, and you looked like you had time on your hands," Sakuya reasoned, shrugging.

"I—I do not have time on my hands. I'll have you know I've been very busy investigating the Dark Lord's identity!" Arle countered.

Unfortunately, the Dark Lord Zol Vadis hadn't contacted the Demon Wolf Pack in the last few days, so her efforts had turned up little.

"Besides, you're the only friend I have who knows this side of me." Sakuya pulled a fox mask from her chest and smiled.

"Wh-what do you mean? W-wait, friend?" Arle's ears perked up.

Sakuya cocked her head. "Aren't we friends?"

"Huh? Hmm... W-well... Yes, I suppose? I guess we are... friends." Arle mouthed the word awkwardly, a blush creeping over her cheeks.

A friend. In all her life, she'd never had anyone she could address as such.

Arle had been chosen at birth by one of the Arc Seven to shoulder the duty of saving the world. Her elf village had left her in the care of the Swordmaster of the Six Heroes.

"W-well, if you need me my help that badly, I suppose I'll escort you..."

"Thank you. I don't know if it's appropriate compensation, but..." Sakuya grinned, pulling a ticket from her pocket and handing it to Arle.

"...What's this?"

"A spectator ticket for the Holy Sword Dance Festival. They gave them out to the participants."

"I can have this?"

"Yes. I'd be glad if you came to watch."

"H-hmph..." Arle eyed the ticket. "I-I'll take it. I'm not sure if I'll be able to attend, however. I mean, I am busy... But we're f-friends... and all..."

The pair continued toward their objective while discussing the upcoming event. They came upon a metallic door blocked behind a few stacked crates of supplies. Loud music, clattering, and shouts were audible from beyond.

"Let's go in..."

Sakuya donned her festival fox mask and stepped inside. The

room past the door was much more spacious than either girl had expected. At one point, it had likely been a supply warehouse. A melody boomed, and a throng of rough-looking people shouted over the noise.

Arle frowned, her long ears flicking. "What a racket. It makes my ears hurt."

Sakuya pushed straight through the crowd, approaching the center of the chamber. There, she and Arle saw a large fighting ring illuminated by many overhead lamps.

This was an underground arena where the city's criminals gathered to test their mettle.

"Oh, what's this? I don't think girlies like you belong here." A werewolf man with sharp claws grabbed Sakuya by the shoulder as she approached the ring.

"I want to fight, too," she replied. "It's open to anyone, isn't it?"

"Stop fooling around, girl! The Black Fangs run this place!" the werewolf snarled at her.

"Activate."

Argent light flashed through the darkness. Sakuya's Raikiri-maru cut the werewolf's whiskers short.

"...What?!" The beastman froze, his eyes wide with astonishment.

The crowd broke into an uproar. Sakuya peered into the ring, Raikirimaru still crackling with lightning.

"Good, there are other Holy Swordsmen here..."

Sakuya's gaze settled on a hulking man with a large broadsword alight with flames. Using Holy Swords in urban spaces was strictly forbidden outside of emergencies. This man may have been a member of some anti-government organization, or perhaps just a combat junkie who wanted the chance to wield his Holy Sword to his heart's content.

Whoever he is doesn't matter to me.

Sakuya stepped onto the ring and readied Raikirimaru. "Now,

which one of you wants to try me first? Or maybe..." She looked down on the people waiting to get into the ring. "You all want to come at me at once? I don't mind..."

◆

A cybernetic Assault Garden, made up of electronic terminals—the Astral Garden. In this infinite space formed by a grid of geometric cubes, the Queen of the Night spread her wings, sailing elegantly through the air.

She wore an alluring black dress that boldly emphasized her cleavage, giving Elfiné an appearance that would shock those who knew her. Elfiné herself had designed this avatar.

I can't let Riselia and the others see me like this.

While she'd worn a witch costume during the Holy Light Festival, Elfiné wanted to don bold, sexy outfits like Riselia and the others more often. How would that boy react if he saw her as the Queen of the Night? Would his heart skip a beat, like when he saw Riselia's provocative costume?

What a silly idea...

Before long, she discovered what she was looking for within the vast sea of information, a black cat hopping from grid to grid.

"Good work, Cait Sith."

It was an Artificial Elemental that Elfiné had created from one of the Eye of the Witch orbs. She'd asked Leonis to slip it into a Phillet-owned casino so that it might infiltrate the establishment's main network. The Phillet Company's base of operations was situated in Camelot's Central Garden, and was supremely well-defended. Accessing records on the business's Artificial Elementals would be challenging, even for Efliné.

Hopefully, this confidential data from my brother's casino will give me a way in, though...

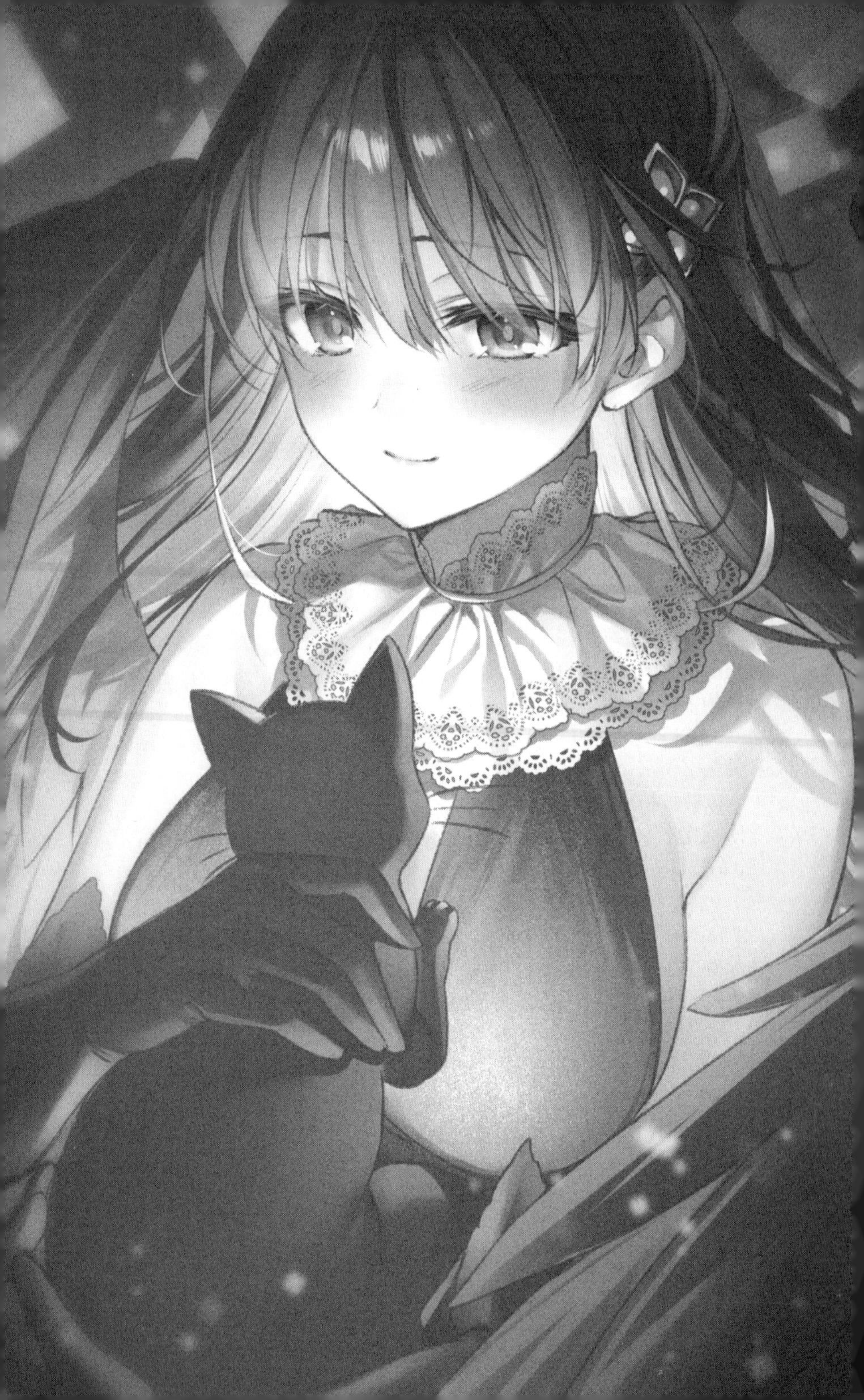

Elfiné cradled the black cat in her arms and accepted the information cube it held. She used the Eye of the Witch to scan it for any viruses, then accessed it carefully. The geometric cube opened up, and data on casino patrons poured into an Eye of the Witch orb.

Elfiné sought information to explain her brother's, Finzel Phillet's, connection to the Demon Sword Project. That wasn't all, however. She was also after anything related to Deinfraude Phillet, her father and the man who killed her mother.

"What's this...?" There was something unusual within the list of customers.

Apparently, priests from the Human Church had visited the casino multiple times. The religion advocated for eliminating the Voids, and although it didn't preach abstinence from vice as it once had, it still felt unusual for a priest to frequent a gambling establishment.

Records indicated multiple people coming and going from the casino, but the names used were clearly aliases.

Is it possible they're all the same person? I might have to look into this.

Elfiné was already aware of the army's involvement in the early stages of the D Project. If the military, the Phillet Company, and the Human Church were all wrapped up in this...

I can't imagine taking this on alone...

She'd set herself up against a massive conspiracy. But was it right to drag Riselia and the others into such a dangerous battle?

Elfiné thought of someone, and she saw a ten-year-old boy's face.

Leo...

By now, Elfiné was confident that he was no mere refugee child. She still had data on him that should have gone to the administrative bureau.

Back when the Void Stampede descended on the Seventh Assault Garden. When the Void Reef vanished. When they engaged that mysterious Void Lord in the Third Assault Garden. And when the Void hive in the ancient ruins was abruptly eradicated...

That ten-year-old boy was always involved somehow. Elfiné didn't know who he really was or what he intended.

Still, he might be able to...

Somewhere, deep down, she carried a kind of expectation of him. Was he this world's hope? Or perhaps he was...

Elfiné's older sister had told her about them way back.

...a Dark Lord. An incarnation of destruction and chaos that burned the ancient world.

"Find anything interesting?" a voice inquired, disrupting Elfiné's contemplation.

"...?!" The girl's eyes widened.

The data cube fizzled away into particles of light and changed shape. Now it looked like a fairy just large enough to rest in Elfiné's hands if she cupped them. It took flight and fluttered over her like a butterfly, its black wings sprinkling luminous motes as they beat.

"What?!" Elfiné called out in alarm.

Did the information cube conceal a backdoor access point?!

"Heh-heh, it's nice to meet you, miss. ♪ I've been dying to!" The fairy stopped in midair and regarded her with a cherubic smile. "My name is Seraphim. I'm a messenger that conveys the voice of the goddess."

"Seraphim...!" Elfiné froze from shock.

She knew that name. She'd been working to discover the truth behind it for some time. An entity called Seraphim had appeared to some of Excalibur Academy's Holy Swordsmen, including Liat Guinness, the captain of the seventh platoon, Elfiné's old unit. Seraphim granted them the power of Demon Swords.

Evidently, Seraphim was a Phillet Company mass-produced Artificial Elemental.

"Oh, you know me already. I'm so happy to hear that." The fairy girl giggled.

"You're the one who gave Liat and the others their Demon Swords, aren't you?"

"Me? No! I'm incapable of producing or granting Demon Swords," Seraphim replied. "All I do is relay the goddess's voice to those who seek power."

"...Goddess?"

Many students who wielded the Demon Swords mentioned hearing the voice of some goddess, but Elfiné had assumed it to be the Artificial Elemental.

"What do you mean? Aren't you the one creating the Demon Swords?" Elfiné questioned.

Seraphim sneered. "You humans know nothing about the Holy Swords. You keep telling yourselves that lie that they come from the planet's power, wielding them without knowing what they actually are."

"What...? Wh-what are you saying?"

"Holy Swords and Demon Swords *are the same, in essence.*" The fairy smiled alluringly and peered into Elfiné's dark eyes. "Tell me, Elfiné Phillet. Don't you desire strength?"

"...What?"

"Open yourself to the goddess's words. If your Holy Sword were to be reborn as a Demon Sword, you'd wield the power of a true witch. And with it, you'd surpass your brother, and even that monster, Count Deinfraude Phillet."

The seductive whisper tickled her earlobe. Was it the fairy who spoke? Or was this irresistible, overwhelming voice perhaps...?

"Stop looking inside my head!" Elfiné glared at the Artificial Elemental. "And don't think you can trick me that easily!"

Her Holy Sword, the Eye of the Witch, loosed a flash that destroyed the grid forming the space around them and triggered a loud alarm.

"Demon Swords can't be allowed to exist, and that goes for the people who create them, too!" Elfiné declared.

"That's a pity," the fairy replied from someplace unseen. "You would've made an excellent witch—maybe even an apostle. Let's meet again someday, shall we? In the goddess's world—"

A single black feather fluttered down to Elfiné's feet.

◆

An upside-down palace floated in the infinite void. This was the Otherworldly Castle, a structure that belonged to one of the eight Dark Lords, Azra-Ael, the Devil of the Underworld. This mobile fortress was the only base in the Dark Lords' Armies' command capable of moving between dimensions.

At present, its owner was absent, and it couldn't travel between planes, but it was still a sturdy bastion. This castle's reception hall, a temple chamber that stood upside down, with a ceiling serving as the floors, was filled to the brim with gigantic eyes.

No, not eyes—jewels. Black gems polished like mirrors. The many eyelike stones reflected the lone visitor to this bizarre chamber. He was a tall man in a classy suit. With such handsome features, one could even call him beautiful.

However, dark madness burned in his eyes.

This was Count Phillet's second son, Finzel Phillet, the leader of the Demon Sword Project and a traitor to humanity.

"Rejoice, ye sly fool of a short-lived race, for your accomplishments have marked you worthy of attending this banquet," declared one of the eyes above him.

"I am honored, apostles of the goddess." He fell prostrate, regarding the echoing voice with awe and respect.

Finzel felt like a cold blade hung above his nape. His life meant nothing to the courtiers of this place.

"You have asked to bask your flesh in the goddess's blessing. To become a Void."

Another spoke from the eyes. It was the clingy, viscous, and stagnant voice of a woman.

"Yes. That is my true wish."

"Should you lend your ear to the goddess's voice and bask in her blessing, you shall cease to be a man and become part of the emptiness that covers all in this world."

"Ooh, what a glorious fate. There is no higher honor for me!" Finzel raised his head and cried out in craving, his eyes fanatical.

"Will you become a traitor to humanity and consign your homeland to be burned away by the Voids?"

"The capital was nothing but a prison to me. My father, my brother, the Holy Swords—none of them acknowledged me. The Assault Gardens, my world, even this despicable human shell! I cast them away without a single regret!"

"Very well."

The eyes overhead gazed down upon the man, and loud laughter filled the inverted chamber.

"Finzel Phillet, he who the goddess guided to betray humankind. We shall grant you the privilege to advance into the deepest depths of the hidden temple to meet our goddess."

"Ohhh...ohhhh! You have my everlasting thanks, gracious apostles!"

"However..." An eye swiveled above the man weeping in gratitude. *"That will only come after you have completed the task the goddess has assigned you."*

Finzel Phillet hung his head. "Yes. Of course. Preparations for the Pseudo-Goddess Creation, the D Project, and the Void Shift are complete. I shall be as your hands and feet, great apostles, and exact the goddess's will."

"The will of the goddess. For this world to be reborn in emptiness."

"The will of the goddess. For this world to be reborn in emptiness," Finzel Phillet echoed, chanting the words as though they were from scripture.

The air around him bent and warped, and his body seemed to fold up and vanish. Silence reigned in the chamber until one of the floating eyes deigned to speak.

"Will he really be of use, old one?"

"Worry not. Even rusted swords have a use. That man would not have advanced the Pseudo-Goddess Creation and the D Project had he lacked devotion."

"But there's still the matter of the rogue Swordmaster. That ceaselessly evolving monster still wanders about, seeking to spill our goddess's blood..."

"The Divine Dragon is tracking Shardark Void Lord."

"The Swordmaster isn't our only problem. There is another out there, an unknown element. They're trying to gather the Dark Lords before we can."

"The fourteenth apostle, Zemein, went to the Undead King's resting place, yet found that his old master was already missing. And Zemein was slain shortly afterward."

"Deviations are appearing in the prophecy."

The space in the center of the room warped, and a figure appeared, a white-haired young man wearing the garb of the Human Church. Nefakess Void Lord, the thirteenth apostle.

He grinned, tapping his staff against the floor. "I just saw your last guest on the way back. He was quite overjoyed at having been granted an audience with the goddess."

"How go your preparations, Lord Nefakess?" a viscous, womanly voice inquired.

"Perfectly. I've already taken care of everything within the Human Church."

"Oh? Good. You can leave the rest to us."

"Of course, Lady Iris."

As Nefakess bowed his head respectfully, one of the eyes overhead changed into particles of light, spreading around the upside-down chamber like grains of sand. The luminous specks coalesced together, assuming the form of a woman.

The stunning beauty had crimson eyes and sleek black hair that trailed to her waist. She wore a pitch-black dress adorned with skulls and a dark robe over it. This was the ninth apostle and leader of the Dark Lords' Armies' Necromancy Unit, Iris Void Priestess.

She had been a commander directly beneath the Undead King, Leonis Death Magnus. And as a dark priestess, she had been entrusted with Roselia Ishtaris's oracle.

She licked her crimson lips and smiled alluringly.

"Heh-heh...I look forward to the moment when a celebration of humanity's hope becomes the day all hell breaks loose."

CHAPTER 5

THREE DARK LORDS IN THE WASTELAND

"Hmmm-hmmm. ♪ Hmm-hm-hmmmm. ♪"

A lovely humming filled the hotel bathroom, with the jovial sounds of splashing water.

It was the morning of the eighteenth platoon's third day in the capital. Shary, back in her natural form for the first time in a while, was enjoying a soak alone.

Normally, she cleansed herself at a spring within the Realm of Shadows. This time, however, she took advantage of the fact that she was staying at a high-class hotel and decided to enjoy the tub in Riselia's room.

"Hmm-hm-hmmm. ♪"

After spending so much time as Leonis yesterday, she felt worn out. Of course, she was honored to serve as his body double, but having to keep up a convincing act was stressful.

Shary stretched her legs to help her stiff calves relax. A sweet aroma wafted from the rose petals scattered in the water. The time before Riselia Crystalia awoke was a brief respite for her.

The speed with which that girl grows is astounding.

It was only a few months ago that Leonis's sorcery made her an undead. She was already mastering second-order offensive spells, an impressive feat, even for a Vampire Queen. Surely the special training from Leonis and the Three Champions of Rognas played a part, but there was no doubting Riselia possessed exceptional raw potential.

Or perhaps it was more accurate to call it raw spirit? Whatever the exercise, Riselia endured, making her a good student. The girl differed drastically from the nobles Shary knew in the Realm of Shadows.

It pains me to admit it, but I can see why my lord is so taken with her.

The training had worn Shary out as well. She had to balance it with investigating the capital, keeping the Demon Wolf Pack under control, and her part-time job at the confectionery.

When my lord returns, I ought to demand donuts as a special reward. O-or maybe a...p-pat on the head?

Shary's cheeks turned red, and she submerged the lower half of her face in the water, blowing bubbles.

My lord, when will you return...?

And that's when...

"Leo? Are you in the bath?"

...Riselia's voice called out from beyond the door.

"...?!" Shary jolted in alarm.

She's up this early?!

Riselia's adaptability was impressive. She'd been sleeping like a baby this time yesterday.

"I-I'll be right out!" Shary changed her voice to Leonis's and stood with a splash.

"Don't worry. I'm just stepping in to take a quick shower."

"O-oh, I see... Wait, what?!"

The sliding door rattled as it opened to reveal a nude Riselia. Her silvery hair wavered in the steam.

"Ah! Ahhhhhh, whyyy?!" Shary exclaimed. "Why did you come in?!"

"...? I always bathe with Leo... Huh?"

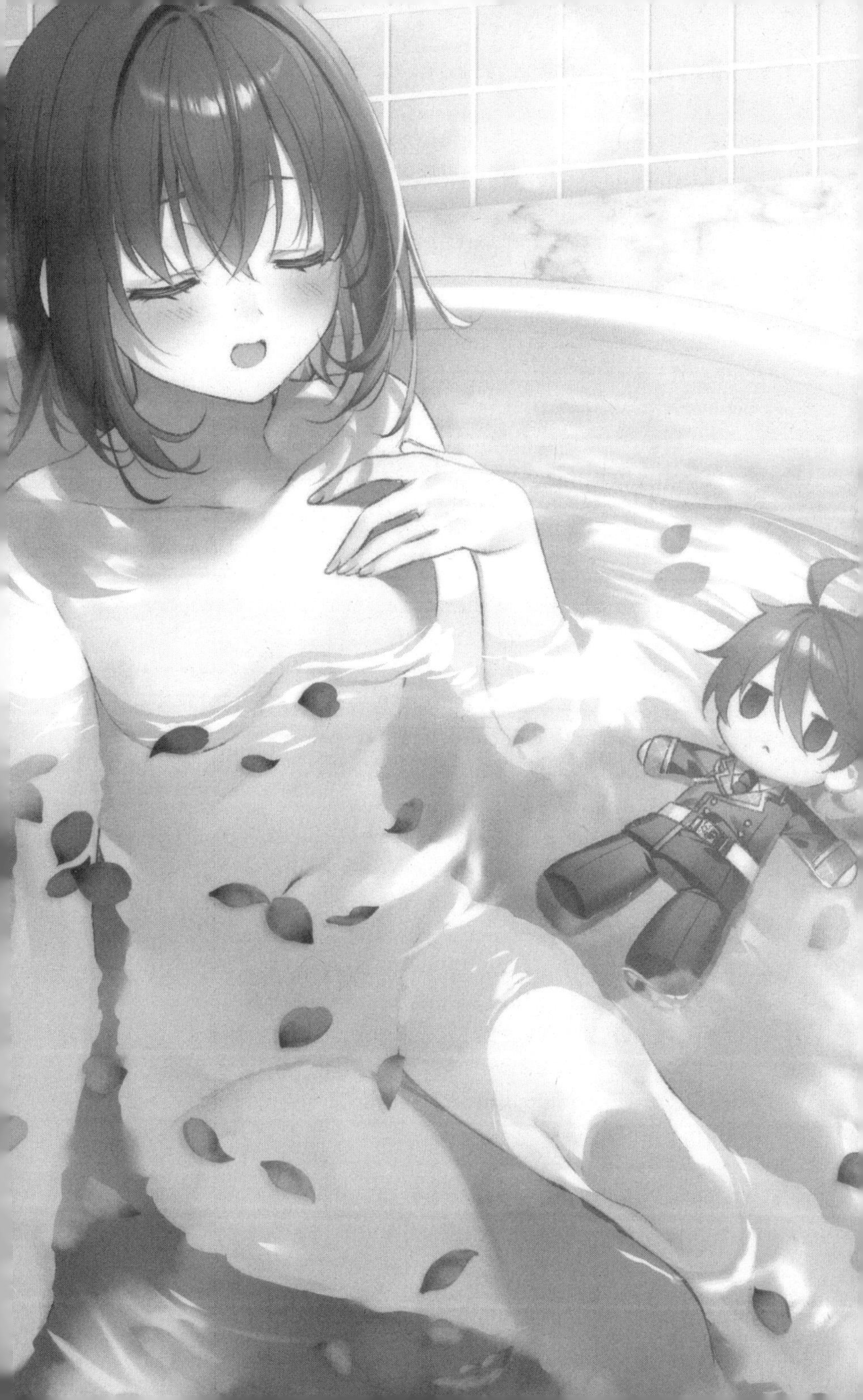

Riselia's ice-blue eyes went wide.

"...A-a girl?!"

Shary grimaced, and she tensed from her spot in the tub.

F-forgive me, my looooord!

...

"Heh-heh. What a surprise. I never imagined you were such a cute girl," Riselia said, turning to look at Shary while tending to her wet hair with a hair dryer.

"What a defeat... I live in the shadows, and yet...," Shary mumbled, sitting on the bed and cradling her head in her hands. Having deemed it pointless to maintain her Leonis facade, she was wearing her usual maid's dress.

I was careless. And I'd kept myself perfectly hidden so far, too...

The truth was that she hadn't kept herself as well concealed as she believed. Shary glanced up at Riselia.

The assassin's way dictates that I have to make her disappear or kill her now that she knows, but... Shary's dusk-colored eyes glinted dangerously.

The Assassination Society she'd once belonged to, Septentrion, had methods of dispatching the undead...but she couldn't eliminate her master's minion.

Uuuugh... My lord is going to be so mad at me... Shary cradled her head again while the sound of the dryer died down.

Riselia approached Shary and peered into her face. "Hmm. We've met somewhere before, right?" she asked.

"I-impossible! I always hide in the shadows."

"I've seen a maid ghost in our dorm a few times."

Shary averted her eyes. "...You were imagining things."

"All right. We'll just leave it at that." Riselia smiled and straightened up, stretching her knees. "Let's get started on our training, *Leo*."

◆

The Dragon Lord, the Lord of the Seas, and the Undead King.

Three of the Dark Lords who had once plunged the world into an age of terror were now soaring above this other world. After flying for the whole night, all they'd learned about this place the Devil of the Underworld had sent them to was that the sky was red.

It had a sun, so there was a visible difference between day and night. However, the view above remained the color of blood, and thick Void miasma brewed behind the dense clouds.

"This is a hellish place," Leonis whispered as he looked down at the surface from atop the skull dragon's back.

In the past, when Leonis warred with the Everdark Queen, he marched his army through the Land of Demise, located deep within the Terminus Mountain Range. But even the Land of Demise, rife with the fog of death, wasn't as desolate as this realm.

This was a world where emptiness ruled all.

Maybe the Voids appearing in our world originate from this one? Leonis posited.

Voids—unknown beings that took the forms of monsters from ages past. If they were born here...

This could be a chance to stomp them out at their source.

Leonis's stomach suddenly grumbled, pulling him out of his thoughts.

"What is it, Leonis? Are you hungry?" Rivaiz Deep Sea asked, tilting her head to one side. "How curious. The Undead King needs to eat like a living person."

Leonis looked back and saw Rivaiz observing him curiously.

"Hmph. And you sea sprites subsist on storing the sea's mana in your bodies, if I recall."

"Indeed. But that's not to say we abstain from food. When the Underwater Stronghold was still intact, I feasted upon the sacrifices made to me by the deep-sea folk."

"Hey, what are you two on about?"

Veira, flying ahead of the skull dragon, dropped her speed and pulled up alongside Leonis.

"Do you not get hungry, dragon girl?"

"Well...come to think of it, it's been three days since I've eaten anything," Veira replied, growling a bit at Rivaiz.

"You didn't eat those monstrosities?"

"...Are you mocking me, Lord of the Seas? Who would eat those things?!"

I do remember you tearing up the Voids with your jaws, though.

Leonis pondered if that counted as eating them. Veira had been flying nonstop since she left the capital. Dark Lords didn't require slumber or food to stay alive, but that didn't make them incapable of resting.

"Hmm. Perhaps we should stop for a break," Leonis suggested.

"I can still keep flying," Veira said.

"Well, I'm quite hungry. I swear, this human body is so inconvenient..."

Leonis stood on the skull dragon's head and used the mystic eye of farsight to observe the surroundings. Through it, he discovered a hill with a commanding view of the surroundings.

"Let's land there."

◆

As night descended upon this other world, the ominous red skies were washed over with black. The three Dark Lords sat atop the barren hill around a campfire of everlasting flame produced by sorcery.

"Leonis, what is this?" Rivaiz asked curiously.

She was holding a can of preserved food that Leonis had produced from the Realm of Shadows.

"This is one embodiment of modern humanity's wisdom,"

Leonis explained, oddly boasting as though it were his own accomplishment while opening another can. "Try eating it. You'll see."

These were military rations provided to investigation teams on Void hive excursions. Before leaving the capital, Leonis separated part of the Realm of Shadows and took it with him, charging Shary with managing the rest in his absence.

Since the capacity of the Realm of Shadows portion Leonis traveled with was limited, he didn't have many rations, but there were enough to last a few days.

The three opened several kinds of cans and placed them before the flickering flames. Boiled white fish, corned beef, cooked beans, pilaf, curry soup, muffins made with dried fruit, bean stew, and pudding.

"Hmm..." Rivaiz used a spoon to taste the corned beef. "I see. It's quite delectable."

"It's tasty but not very filling," Veira added from her spot on the ground. "I wonder if we couldn't find a cow or three somewhere around here."

Leonis's head perked up. "Oh. So dragons eat cattle?"

"Yeah. We burn down mountains with our fire breath and pick whichever cows were roasted the finest."

"Leviathans can swallow whales whole," Rivaiz noted.

"Whales are delicious, too," Veira replied. "I can't swallow one whole, though."

Leonis observed the other Dark Lords' discussion with exasperation. "Forget cows. I don't think we'll find anything alive here save for the Voids," he said.

And he couldn't say if those monstrosities of the emptiness even counted as living beings. Rivaiz suddenly glanced over at Leonis.

"I believe it's my first time seeing you eat, Undead King," she said.

"I'm used to it by now," Leonis stated as he chewed on his roasted beans.

He didn't much care for the food, but a certain minion girl always scolded him when he neglected to eat his vegetables.

"Hmm, I see." Rivaiz nodded, watching in fascination as Leonis ate the canned food. "Still, I did not expect a master sorcerer like you to fail a reincarnation spell."

"...Mind your own business," Leonis shot back.

"You were originally undead, after all. You did not need to reincarnate, so why did you not simply slumber for a thousand years?"

"I couldn't do that. I was a special undead, created by the goddess."

And what's more, the goddess had instructed him to use sorcery to reincarnate. When Roselia Ishtaris raised the hero Leonis Shealto as an undead, his human soul was placed in an undead body. However, his hero soul couldn't acclimate to that new form, meaning it would wear away with time.

Regardless, there was merit to Rivaiz's inquiry. Leonis looked down and sighed. It may have been a highly advanced, twelfth-order spell, but Leonis still had trouble accepting he'd failed. If he'd had no choice but to reincarnate as a human, he would have preferred a slightly older body, if nothing else. Had he been reborn in his prime as the hero, Riselia and Regina wouldn't treat him like a child.

◆

After finishing their dinner of canned food, the three began discussing what to do next.

"We have no idea where that man is." Leonis crossed his arms, looking up to the stars twinkling in the night sky.

They still had no grasp on how large this world was, either. Going after their target without any clues would be difficult.

The only thing we have to go on is the Azure Hold...

"'This structure is the original template of the human cities. A gate with which to reach the stars.'"

What did that man mean when he said that? Wasn't the Azure Hold just a flying fortress?

"Veira, did you know the Azure Hold could traverse dimensions?"

"N-no, I didn't know anything about that." The Dragon Lord looked away and sulked for some reason. "The Azure Hold was discovered in the depths of the earth by the great dragon elders generations before me. They investigated its functions and realized it was capable of flying."

"And you used it as your stronghold despite knowing nothing about who constructed it?" Rivaiz knit her brow, exasperated.

"The great dragons don't mind little details like that!"

"Maybe you should start minding them, then," Leonis whispered, his eyes narrowed.

"I admit that the Azure Hold possesses mysterious ancient mechanisms that we dragons couldn't fully comprehend. One was the Almagest, an astronomical observation device that recorded the movements of the stars."

Leonis was aware of the device. Veira had searched for the Azure Hold on the ocean floor because she wanted to use the Almagest to observe the changes in the stars' positions.

"A gate with which to reach the stars," he said, Leonis recalled.

"I think it's safe to say that man knew the Azure Hold's original purpose."

"Just who was that human...?" Veira growled bitterly.

Come to think of it, I still haven't told them.

"I think it's likely he's the Devil of the Underworld, Azra-Ael."

"What?!" Veira exclaimed.

Rivaiz's eyes betrayed her disbelief.

"I have no real proof. This is only speculation," Leonis prefaced before explaining his reasoning. And once he'd finished...

"I see. Yes, there were times when the Devil of the Underworld possessed human bodies." Veira nodded, convinced.

As a spiritual life-form, Azra-Ael had to claim the flesh of another living being to maintain their form. The body didn't have to be human, although it seemed the Devil of the Underworld preferred them.

"So assuming that man is Azra-Ael... What does he hope to achieve by using the Azure Hold and the Dark Lords?" Rivaiz wondered.

Leonis shook his head. "Who can say?"

Had he known, it still wouldn't complete the picture. He kept this from the other two Dark Lords, but...

He's possessing the body of Riselia's father, Duke Crystalia.

That couldn't be a coincidence. There was undoubtedly a reason.

Duke Crystalia had been investigating the Dark Lords, too...

He'd been looking into legends surrounding the supposedly deceased Dark Lords and had even deciphered part of the ancient text. Thanks to that, Riselia translated an epitaph that nearly exposed Leonis's true identity.

Did Duke Crystalia summon Azra-Ael in some way?

In which case, was Duke Crystalia still acting of his own free will...?

He used the power of a Holy Sword, but...

Holy Swords were a power exclusive to humans. Was possession of a body enough to use one freely?

"...Leo?" Veira eyed the boy dubiously.

"There's no point in trying to discern his goals without all the information," Leonis decided. "We have to capture him."

"Yes, I suppose you're right...," Veira agreed, spreading her shapely legs on the ground. "But there's a chance he went back to our old world all on his own."

"No, I don't think that's likely," Leonis stated, looking up. "Even the Devil of the Underworld can't travel between dimensions that easily. Crossing alone wouldn't be too difficult for him, but transporting the Azure Hold will require considerable preparation. Even the Otherworldly Castle, feared for its capability to appear anywhere, couldn't move between worlds effortlessly."

"Either way, we need to find him, and fast," Veira concluded.

"Right..."

Leonis reached out for the night sky, eyes fixed upon it. He reached toward the sky of another world, where the positions of the stars were different.

How strange...

Somehow, his thoughts wandered to the minion girl he'd left behind in the capital. Should he tell her that Lord Crystalia, her father, was still alive...?

He longed to hear her voice. To feel the embrace of her arms, her fingers brushing through his hair.

Absurd. This is almost like... My word, how irksome...

Leonis closed his eyes. Was Shary doing well as his body double? He trusted her but couldn't shake his concern.

❖

"Today's training is complete!"

Riselia returned to the entrance of the park, breathing heavily. "...Already?" She looked up at Shary, disguised as Leonis. She glanced at the shadow hourglass sitting on a nearby bench, but only half the darkness within it had fallen to the bottom. Riselia had finished much sooner than on her first day. Perhaps her body was getting accustomed to outputting the right amount of mana.

She really is a Vampire Queen. This kind of potential is hard to come by. Shary tapped her replica of the Staff of Sealed Sins against the ground. "Very well. Let's move on to the next step in your training," she stated.

"The next step?" Riselia asked.

"Controlling your mana."

"O-okay!" Riselia nodded vigorously. Unfortunately, she'd expended most of her mana and couldn't get up.

After a moment of thought, Shary said, "Before we do, however, I'll give you special permission to suck my blood." She held out a finger to Riselia, still on the ground.

"...Are you sure?"

"You won't be able to continue training with your mana depleted."

"Okay. Then..." Riselia gulped and plopped Shary's fingertip into her mouth.

"Ow... Hey, you're sucking too much!"

"Ah, I-I'm sorry... I can't really help it..."

"...Nngh, l-learn some restraint."

"But Leo always lets me suck more."

"...H-he just pampers you too much," Shary huffed, placing a hand on her waist. Riselia continued nibbling on her finger, however. "Nnh... Ah... Nff..." Shary, in Leonis's form, let out wanton moans.

Eventually, Riselia's argent hair began glowing faintly with mana.

"Y-you've had enough, right?" Shary asked.

"Y-yes... Thank you." Riselia looked unsatisfied, but Shary couldn't afford to have her take any more blood.

Shary cleared her throat. "Then let's begin improving your mana control. You are a Vampire Queen, the strongest kind of undead."

"...I—I am?" Riselia asked, confused.

"Yes. Honestly, in terms of sheer mana, your capacity is already greater than mine by now."

"Are you saying I can become as strong as Leo?" Riselia questioned, ice-blue eyes wide with amazement.

"Don't get carried away." Shary struck Riselia over the head with her staff.

"Ow!"

"Our master is on a whole different level. If I were to compare you two, he is the sun and you are a mosquito."

"A mosquito..." Riselia stiffened up as if the word had stunned her emotionally. "It's not like I'm that indiscriminate when sucking blood..."

Shary ignored Riselia's meek protest and carried on. "I want you to call upon the True Ancestor's Dress."

"...Huh? But I just replenished all my mana. Wouldn't that just deplete it all again?"

"Yes, it would. And that's the point."

"...?"

"As you are now, you haven't fully drawn out the true power of the True Ancestor's Dress. It devours the wearer's mana to strengthen their body but can also circulate mana to intensify the strength of your spells several times over."

"H-hmm..."

"I see you don't quite understand. Very well." Shary sighed and shrugged. "For now, just dress up."

"Dress up... F-fine." Riselia nodded, took a deep breath, and focused the mana in her body.

Magical energy ran and raged, and a crimson dress, as red as blood, manifested and enveloped her body.

"Her mana really is overwhelming...," Shary whispered.

"I...can't really maintain this state...for long...," Riselia confessed with a pained expression as she collapsed to her knees. Her mana would deplete entirely in less than a minute, and she'd lose consciousness.

"Remain in this state and try circulating the mana inside your body."

"I—I can't... The way I am now, it's...impossible..." Riselia moaned in pain.

Her ice-blue eyes glinted as an insuppressible craving for blood overwhelmed her.

"Oh, fine." Shary took a step forward and...jabbed Riselia on the forehead with an index finger.

"Ow!" Riselia exclaimed. "Wh-what did you do that for?!"

"I poked a pressure point to focus your mana. It's normally used as an assassination technique, though..."

"A-assassination?"

"It's a technique called the Death Knell. It kills the target by poking a point where mana converges."

"Huh?!" Riselia screeched.

"Don't worry. You're already dead," Shary stated nonchalantly.

"Erm..."

"More importantly, focus your mana in your forehead."

"O-okay..." Riselia nodded, closed her eyes, and concentrated on her aching forehead.

Her Vampire Queen's immense power gathered there. Before long, the mana raging inside her like a storm began circulating through her body.

"That's right, maintain this state awhile longer."

"Kuh... A-all right... Aah..."

Riselia's silver hair glowed brightly, and her eyes turned crimson. After a few more seconds passed, however...

"U-ugh...I...I can't...keep going..."

...the True Ancestor's Dress fluttered, mana billowing out of it like fire.

"Ngh, ah, ahh..." Roselia returned to her training attire and collapsed limply.

Shary bent down. "Well done. It's always like that at first. We'll add this to your regular training regimen for the remaining days leading up to the festival. I want you to keep circulating your mana at all times, not just during practice, so you'll grow acclimated to how it feels."

Riselia said nothing. She'd completely lost consciousness.

"—I guess you do have some guts after all." Shary shrugged and lifted Riselia in her arms.

◆

Standing in the Central Garden's administrative sector was one building with a characteristically octagonal roof. This was the St. Eluminas Monastery, a Holy Swordsman training school managed by the Human Church, the state religion of the Integrated Empire.

It was much smaller than the Seventh Assault Garden's Excalibur Academy or the Second Assault Garden's Military Instruction School, and maintained a policy to train only a select few. The Holy Swordsmen who graduated from the Monastery were all skilled warriors who fought on the front lines.

At the very center of the octagonal building was the Cathedral Hall, where a group of four was gathered. These students, clad in pure white, were the representatives who would participate in the Holy Sword Dance Festival. Each of them was an elite with a powerful Holy Sword and abundant combat experience against the Voids.

Yet there was no light in their eyes whatsoever. They stood as still as the dead. Their Holy Swords and zealous faith in the Human Church, the things that gave them their identities, had vanished.

"I hand-picked them personally. What do you think?" the white-haired young bishop asked with a grin, his head bowed to the woman standing before the cathedral's altar.

"Why does that matter? They're all just puppets for us." Iris Void Priestess was clad in a pitch-black dress, which clashed with the cathedral's brighter atmosphere. She beheld the young men and women as if appraising prey, before settling her gaze on a petite girl. "But yes, I suppose. A girl with a lovely appearance will do quite well."

Iris raised the girl's chin up, examining her like a jewel. After nodding in satisfaction, she leaned in and then...sank her fangs into the girl's throat.

"Ah! Ahhhh... Ah... Ahhhh..." The girl raised her voice for the first time. Her hands fell limply at her sides, and she looked overcome with rapture. She fully accepted this act of vampirism. The color drained from her youthful features, her skin dried, and she swiftly became a puppet of skin and bone.

"Mmm... Mha... That was quite delicious."

The girl's body, limbs now thin like twigs, toppled to the floor. Having had her fill of blood, Iris licked her lips. And then...

...transformed into the girl whose blood she'd taken.

CHAPTER 6

VOID GODDESS

"Leo...Leonis..."

He heard a voice. A nostalgic one, the one he always yearned for—*her* voice.

"—came...for me...Leonis..."

"Rose...lia...?"

He couldn't see anything. Leonis reached out, his hands groping through the infinite darkness. His fingers caught nothing, however.

"I'm right here. Always, always by your side... That's why, Leonis... Hurry...and find me..."

Leonis awoke.

"Nng..."

He sat up, rubbing his eyelids. His hair was messy and stood on end. No matter how much Leonis tried to stave it off with sheer willpower, his ten-year-old body required sleep. And it seemed he'd grown weary after eating.

It's been a while since I dreamed of her. Leonis shook his head slowly and got up.

Dawn had yet to break. The magical campfire was still burning.

Leonis turned around, feeling a gaze on him. Rivaiz was squatting down next to him, peering closely.

"Wh-what are you doing?!" he exclaimed in surprise.

"Seeing the Undead King slumber so innocently is a rare sight. What's more, you were mumbling in your sleep."

"...?!"

"You were cute, Leo. See?" Veira said, smiling impishly from the other side of the campfire. She held up Leonis's terminal, which displayed a photo of him sleeping.

"G-give that back!" Leonis flushed and snatched the device out of the Dragon Lord's hand.

Veira giggled, got to her feet, and extinguished the magical fire. "We should set out before dawn," she said.

"Right..." Leonis nodded bitterly and reached for the Staff of Sealed Sins, which he had leaned against a rock. No sooner had he done so, however...

Vrrrrrrrrrrrrrrrrrrrrrrr...!

...than the Staff of Sealed Sins let out a high-pitched sound, resonating with something.

"Wh-what?!" Leonis stared at the rod in surprise. He realized it wasn't the staff, but the goddess's Demon Sword, Dáinsleif, sheathed within. "What is this...?"

The sound of the resonance wasn't dying down. And suddenly, Leonis heard a voice in his mind.

"You have come...my dear...child..."

"You kept...your promise..."

"U-ugh...!"

"Ah, Leo, what's wrong?!"

"What's happened?"

Veira and Rivaiz looked confused.

"Roselia..."

"Huh...?"

"I heard...Roselia's voice..." Leonis grabbed the Staff of Sealed Sins and looked intuitively in the direction of the voice—a mountain range stretching out at the end of the wasteland. "It's coming from that direction."

♦

"What do you mean, you heard the goddess's voice?" Veira pressed while flying through the darkness.

"...I don't know. However, the Demon Sword is definitely resonating with her," Leonis answered from atop the skull dragon.

Roselia hadn't spoken to him since reaching out at the camp, yet the Staff of Sealed Sins still hummed in his grip. Dáinsleif reacted once before, in the ruined city, when he saw the Holy Woman of the Six Heroes, Tearis Resurrectia. The Holy Woman hadn't been Roselia's true reincarnation but had harbored some aspect of the goddess.

So why did the Demon Sword respond now, in this other world?

The three Dark Lords crossed the swordlike spires of the mountain range and discovered that a vast forest lay beyond.

"So this world has forests, too," Leonis remarked.

"Hmm, but this place...," Rivaiz whispered.

"Yes," Leonis replied. "It's dead."

The woods beneath them were polluted with Void miasma, and there were no signs of life. However, the trees seemed to writhe, as though the forest had become a Void itself...

"Leo, look at that!" Veira called out. "There are ruins down there!"

Leonis used a Farsight spell to follow Veira's gaze. Between the dead timbers and the deathly fog was a crumbling, stonework fortress. Trees coiled around it, digging into the remains.

Leonis could scarcely believe his eyes. "That's... But wait, that can't be true!" he cried. He recognized this decrepit structure.

"What's wrong, Undead King?" Rivaiz asked him.

"That's the Lord of the Beasts'...Gazoth Hell Beast's Ironblood Castle!"

"What?!"

◆

In the depths of boundless darkness, where the flow of time stood still, the Void King hailed as a hero in ancient times awakened from sleep.

His rousing was an unexpected one. The injuries he'd sustained from the last battle had yet to heal fully, and he was meant to slumber for a while longer.

However, he heard *her* voice.

The voice of his nemesis, the goddess.

"Hrohhh, hrohh, hrohhhhhhhhhhhhhhhhhhh!"

The Void King's howl tore through the darkness.

◆

Gazoth Hell Beast, the Lord of Beasts. He was the destructive master of the Dark Lords' Armies' third division, the Demon Beast Corps, and fought personally on the front lines. Gazoth's stronghold was built in a key location for the conquest of the human kingdom and was the Dark Lords' Armies' greatest fortification.

Yet even it was lost during the war's final days, thanks to a coordinated attack by the Six Heroes. The Lord of Beasts himself dueled the Swordmaster, and although he perished, his demise befitted a Dark Lord.

Standing before the remains of the now-ruined Ironblood Castle, Leonis gasped.

"...There's no mistaking it. This is the Lord of Beasts' fortress."

The moss-covered walls had collapsed and were now half submerged into the ground. Still, Leonis was certain this was Ironblood Castle, for he'd visited it many times as an ally.

"So that's what it looked like," Veira, who had returned to her humanoid form, said. "Gazoth's castle, huh?" She seemed to be confused by this sight.

Admittedly, Leonis wasn't faring much better. "What's going on? Isn't this supposed to be a different world?!"

Why were ruins from a thousand years ago, from Leonis's era, in a place like this?

Maybe we didn't traverse dimensions, but were simply thrown to some other part of our own world?

It was possible, but Leonis found that unlikely. The blood-colored sky and desolate land covered in Void miasma felt too different from home.

Rivaiz cocked her head. "Hmm, this is incomprehensible..."

"Let's just go inside for the time being," Veira decided, taking a light step and then shattering the crumbled walls with a loud kick.

Unlike the exterior facade, the castle's interior had maintained much of its original form. The kingdom's allied forces had stormed these halls and likely sought to use the structure as their frontline base rather than destroy it. Humans might have used it for centuries after it was seized. Parts of the stone showed signs of repair.

A few spots on the walls still emit mana, too, Leonis noticed. Maybe that was why the degradation inside wasn't as severe.

"Is this where the Lord of Beasts died?" Rivaiz asked.

"No, after Ironblood Castle fell, Gazoth Hell Beast challenged the Swordmaster to a duel on the Blood Fang Plains, where they supposedly perished."

"I see. If their remains were here, I would have liked to take them with us."

"If there were any bones around, I'd claim them for my own," Leonis insisted. "I'd love nothing more than to have the Lord of the Beasts' skeleton for my collection."

He considered going to the Blood Fang Plains for them, but now wasn't the time for it. The Staff of Sealed Sins was still resonating in his hand. It felt like the deeper they advanced into the castle, the stronger the reaction.

Is it Roselia?

Leonis produced a flame at the tip of his rod, illuminating the passage leading under the castle.

Why was the Demon Sword reacting to something that resided in another dimension? And how had Ironblood Castle come to rest here?

I have to catch Azra-Ael and get answers out of him.

After descending deep underground, the three Dark Lords came to a giant gate. It was closed shut and sealed firmly with sorcery for good measure. Leonis held up the Staff of Sealed Sins against the gate, realizing that the resonance grew more intense when he did.

He ran his fingers over the walls, analyzing the sorcery used there.

"Sealing magic... And it's not the work of the Lord of Beasts from what I can tell," Leonis remarked.

The spell possessed multiple layers, and as Leonis drew a symbol to undo it...

"This is taking too long. Hyah! Dragon Lord Slash!" Veira suddenly kicked the door.

Bwoosh!

The gigantic barricade was blown away and shattered with a thundering noise. A cloud of dust blew into the air, obfuscating the way forward.

"...That's barbaric, Veira," Leonis chided her.

"Dragons hate dawdling." Veira shrugged.

"On this matter, we are in agreement," Rivaiz said.

The three Dark Lords looked past the door.

"...?!"

The cloud of dust cleared, revealing a pitch-black crystal pyramid that reflected no light.

"...A Goddess Temple?!"

It wasn't anywhere near as big as the one in Necrozoa's underground temple. It was about as large as a casket. A Goddess Temple was a device the Dark Lords' Armies used to receive the goddess's prophecies.

"Now, this is curious...," Rivaiz whispered. "What is a Goddess Temple doing here?"

"I'm not sure...," Leonis replied.

There was a Goddess Temple in every Dark Lords' Armies base, and that included Ironblood Castle, of course. However, the human alliance army destroyed all the ones they came across as they claimed locations during the war. All the temples were annihilated save the one hidden in Necrozoa.

There shouldn't have been one here.

"Maybe the Devil of the Underworld created this altar," Rivaiz suggested.

Leonis nodded. "...Yes. That's possible."

Azra-Ael was devoted to Roselia, so it wouldn't have been too strange to learn they'd built a new one.

"But I still have to wonder what Ironblood Castle is doing here."

"Indeed."

Leonis took a step forward and touched the surface of the black crystal. The Demon Sword contained inside the Staff of Sealed Sins reacted violently. In response, the black crystal released a flash, followed by...

<—nd...my beloved...child...>

...a voice.

◆

"What...?"

Leonis wasn't the only one who'd heard it, either. Rivaiz and Veira acknowledged static-laden words echoing from every direction. The black crystal flickered again.

<—found you...beloved child...successor to...Demon Sword...>

The barely intelligible voice echoed through the chamber. The Demon Sword in Leonis's hands hummed in concert.

<Why...? I thought you had...disappeared...from this world...>

"I...disappeared?" Leonis whispered, dumbfounded. "What are you saying? Who are you?!" His shout drowned out the strange, garbled speaker.

It couldn't possibly be *her*. The goddess had perished long ago, to be reincarnated into a human body a thousand years later. Yet against all logic, Leonis believed this voice to be hers.

When Zemein activated the Goddess Temple in Necrozoa, Dáinsleif hadn't responded like this. Therefore, this speaker had to be someone else who'd assumed the goddess's identity.

Surely, that was it, yet Leonis knew on instinct that this was no pretender. It was definitely *her*...

<...I've always looked for you...>

This voice from the black crystal...

<...Always sought you out...>

<Always, always, always, alwaysalwaysalways...>

...kept repeating the word with maddened, yearning desire.

"Roselia...is it...really you?" Leonis whispered, voice tense.

He reached out for the crystal like she was truly there.

<...My beloved child, successor to the Demon Sword...I've always...waited for...you... Please...you must...find me...>

"Roselia! I'm here! I'm right here!" Leonis couldn't help but shout. He beat his hand against the pyramid repeatedly. "Roselia!"

Veira grabbed his arm. "Leo! Something's wrong!"

"What...?" The Dragon Lord's alarmed expression helped Leonis calm down.

<I...am...■to...■■■■■■■■...■■■...>

The goddess's voice changed suddenly. Black mist bled from the crystal, surrounding Leonis's hands.

"What?!" He pulled away, assailed by a terrible sensation, like his soul was beginning to fester.

Void miasma...?

The vapor coiled around his arms, climbing up to his neck slowly.

<...My dear...child...■■■■ Star of...Nothingness...■■■■...>

"Ro...selia...!" Leonis moaned.

"Hahhhhhhhhhh!" Veira cried, slamming her fist against the Goddess Temple.

A crack ran through its obsidian surface, and it shattered with a loud, clear sound.

"Veira, what did you do?!" Leonis shouted, not immediately aware of how loud he'd spoken.

The Dragon Lord didn't pay it much mind, however, staring at her fellow Dark Lord. "Leo, your hand...!" She stared at Leonis's arm.

"What...is this?!"

The places where the miasma had touched Leonis's right hand

were inflamed as though from a burn, and a strange pattern formed on his arm. A sharp, burning pain ran through his skin.

"It looks like a hex," Rivaiz stated while examining the marking.

"A hex...?"

Rivaiz frowned, observing it closely. "Yes. I've never seen such a pattern before, though..."

The crushed remains of the Goddess Temple were beginning to lose their glow.

"Let's get out of here for the time being," Veira said. "I can't say I like the air of this place."

"I am in agreement," Rivaiz added. She picked up a black fragment. "For now, I'll take this back with us."

"Ugh, wait, something's...coming!" Leonis called. He spoke entirely out of intuition. Every cell in his body shrieked in alarm.

This feeling... No, it can't be... Is it really him?!

The Dragon Lord and Lord of the Seas noticed the presence at the same time.

"Wh-what?!"

"This is...?"

They looked up to the ceiling. And the moment they did...

Crrrraaaaaaash!

...Ironblood Castle was utterly erased.

CHAPTER 7

THE VOID KING

The air wavered from the sheer heat. Bits of flame smoldered at the edge of the miasma forest. The site of Ironblood Castle was now a gigantic crater, a spear at its center.

A single spear had destroyed the entire area.

The three Dark Lords stood a short distance from the point of impact, a dome-shaped barrier surrounding them.

"Had that been a direct hit, I don't think my spell would have managed to block it," Leonis said, holding up the Staff of Sealed Sins.

"Is that...a spear?" Veira asked.

"I sense a vast amount of mana coming from it," Rivaiz whispered, fascinated. "This seems to be a weapon of the gods."

Remnants of stone walls littered the blasted ground. The Goddess Temple had been eradicated.

Brionac, the Divine Spear. Only he *is capable of throwing such a weapon.*

Leonis turned his attention to the sky. Shining within the fathomless dark was a gigantic, grotesque form. The Void King floated overhead, countless Voids waiting upon him.

"So fate has led us to meet again..." Leonis glared at the fallen hero. "My teacher, Shardark the Swordmaster."

"...Shardark?!" Veira's golden eyes shot wide. "Leo, what do you mean? Is that really the Swordmaster of the Six Heroes?"

Leonis nodded, feeling a bead of cold sweat slide down his neck. Shardark Shin Ignis, a Void Lord who commanded the Voids. His form had changed since the clash in the Seventh Assault Garden.

After absorbing gods and demons, he became a malformed monster. His lower half had swelled, sprouting eight legs, each belonging to a different creature. Likewise, eight hands had grown from his upper half, each wielding a mythology-class weapon.

The only part of this terrifying living nightmare that still bore any resemblance to the man he was once was his pale, handsome face. However, one of his eyes was crushed, the remnants of an injury Leonis had inflicted.

...What is he doing here?

The Swordmaster had descended upon the Seventh Assault Garden as a Void Lord to fuse with a Sakura Orchid guardian deity. After a fierce battle with Leonis, he'd retreated into a tear in space when Leonis had awakened to the power of his Holy Sword and shot him between the eyes.

So if he's here after disappearing into that fracture in reality...

It seemed Leonis's hypothesis that the Voids originated from this world was correct. That was a major piece of information about the otherwise completely unknown creatures.

Now's hardly the time to celebrate that, though.

Leonis raised the Staff of Sealed Sins. "That is definitely the Swordmaster of the Six Heroes. After succumbing to the emptiness and becoming the Void Lord, he's been indiscriminately fusing with any being he's deemed worthy."

"Shardark Shin Ignis!" Veira growled, her voice thick with

bloodlust. Her draconic golden eyes glinted menacingly. Hundreds of her dragons had perished at this hero's hands.

"What is the Swordmaster doing here?" Rivaiz inquired calmly.

"I don't know."

Had this fallen hero been drawn by the goddess's voice? Or perhaps it was a result of Dáinsleif's resonance...?

"■■■■■■■■■■■...!" Shardark Void Lord's howl shook the air.

"Here he comes!" Leonis shouted.

Whoooosh!

The Swordmaster's gigantic form descended like a comet, blasting another, smaller crater into the earth.

"Eighth-order gravity spell—Vira Zuo!"

Vnnnnn!

A sphere of gravity formed in the air, flattening the Swordmaster against the ground. But that was all it accomplished. Even the strongest gravity spell could only momentarily stall him.

"I'll crush you with one blow—Drag Zelga!"

"Wintertide of swords, frozen blades of demonic ice—Sharianos!"

Veira chanted a spell in the dragon tongue while Veira cast an eighth-order ice spell. A spiraling force that dug into the ground and a storm of whirling ice blades enveloped the Swordmaster's gigantic body. The maelstrom of the Dark Lords' powers blew away the surrounding Voids in an instant.

"Even the strongest of the Six Heroes can't hope to face three Dark Lords at once... What?!" Veira's confident smile faded swiftly.

"■■■■—■■■■■■■...!"

Shardark swung one of his arms, brushing away the dust around him with a massive hammer, a mythology-class weapon. He hurled the hammer effortlessly. No ordinary defensive spell could block it.

THE DEMON SWORD MASTER OF EXCALIBUR ACADEMY, VOL. 8

"Come forth from the shadows, cadavers of the Realm of Shadows—Great Death Wall!"

Countless bones reinforced by mana assembled to form a thick wall of bones. This was an original spell of the Undead King's, which didn't exist in the magic system. However, the spinning mallet broke through each layer of the barricade, speeding toward Leonis.

My precious bones!

Before Leonis had time to lament the loss, the great hammer was upon him.

"Hahhhhhhhhh! Drag Fist!"

Veira threw a punch charged with mana, which smashed against the mallet's side and knocked it off course. It raced past Leonis, barely missing his face, and slammed into the ground with a thunderous noise.

"What a monster... Just knocking it aside took all I had..."

"And that's after the bone wall dampened so much of its momentum. He's more powerful than he ever was in life," Leonis said.

"And sorcery hardly affects him, too," Rivaiz pointed out.

"Indeed." Leonis nodded. "Shardark couldn't use sorcery in life. He was focused purely on swordsmanship. But by evolving, he absorbed gods capable of wielding holy magic."

He'd blocked Veira and Rivaiz's onslaught with a holy spell.

My old teacher, you once called me a monster for becoming the Undead King, but you have become more monstrous than I ever was. Leonis scowled.

Had the three Dark Lords been at their full strength, they would have destroyed this pest effortlessly. But the strongest of them, the Lord of the Seas, had lost her other half, the leviathan.

Leonis was in a ten-year-old's body, reducing his physical

prowess and cutting his mana to a third of its original capacity. Donning Blackas in his Black Tyrant form would help, but he couldn't summon his brother-in-arms from the Realm of Shadows right now.

The only one who could manage a decent fight was Veira, the Dragon Lord. But even in her case, her attacks were primarily magical in nature, making her ill-suited to face the Swordmaster. And a dragon's innate spell resistance was nearly meaningless against Shardark.

We need to retreat, but turning our backs on him won't be wise...

Leonis didn't feel that knowing when to flee besmirched a Dark Lord's honor. After all, it was only through countless defeats that the Undead King had found the path to supremacy. Unfortunately, retreating here would be too risky. If they tried, one of the three Dark Lords—Leonis, Veira, or Rivaiz—would surely be slain.

Besides, while Leonis didn't see fleeing as disgraceful, the Dragon Lord and the Lord of the Seas might be too proud to run.

The Void King roared and charged toward them. With his eight legs, stolen from gods and devils, he kicked away the remnants of Ironblood Castle, his every step a thunderclap.

"Leo. I'll stall him, so cover for me," Veira said with a ferocious smile before shifting into her true form.

"Graaaaaaaaah...!"

A gigantic crimson dragon appeared, enveloped in crimson flames, and met the Swordmaster's charge.

Thud!

The collision sent a shock wave radiating out in every direction. Dirt blew into the air, forcing Leonis to shield his face from the debris. Grappling her opponent head-on, Veira parted her jaws and exhaled sizzling dragon breath at point-blank range!

The red flames consumed Shardark's upper half. His divine

protection didn't trigger. The dragon's claws tore into the Swordmaster's flesh.

Despite being struck directly and exposed to the incandescent fire, the Swordmaster refused to stop. He used the great shield he carried to slam the red dragon's head, knocking her back.

Shardark hurled a greatsword.

"Sharia Sheiz!"

A blade of water lanced from the distance, severing Shardark's fingers.

"We're hunting big game here. We must attack it from three directions!" Rivaiz called out as she flew through the air.

Leonis sprinted along the ground, chanting an advanced spell.

If only I could use the Demon Sword, I'd be able to defeat him.

Dáinsleif remained locked within the staff, unstirring. Shardark had absorbed one of the Dark Lords, and owing to the oath Leonis had made with the goddess, he was unable to wield Dáinsleif's power against one of his fellow Dark Lords.

The Demon Sword isn't my only trump card, but...

As he raced through the wasteland, Leonis unintentionally clenched his right hand. His Holy Sword, Excalibur XX—Leonis had manifested that unknown power once before to defeat Shardark Void Lord. It wasn't a power he could use freely, however. Much like Dáinsleif, it consumed all his mana and stamina, so he could fire it only in all-or-nothing situations.

"Ye who consume life, I offer my soul as a sacrifice to beckon you—Skull Colossus!"

The shattered bones scattered on the ground clattered and writhed, converging before Leonis. They came together, forming a thirty-melte-tall sculpture made of bone.

"It's delightful, looking down upon my teacher like this..." Leonis smiled viciously, sitting atop the construct's hand. He gazed below at Shardark, who was still grappling with the red dragon. "Holy Sword, Excalibur XX—Activate!" Leonis chanted the words while focusing on his fingertips.

Particles of light converged, manifesting to form a Holy Sword shaped like a pistol. Yet not a moment later, black sparks shot from his right hand. Pain ran through Leonis's body, and the half-manifested Holy Sword dispersed.

"...What?!" Leonis grimaced and looked down at his hand. The strange pattern Rivaiz called a hex surfaced on his skin.

Has it sealed my Holy Sword?!

Leonis tried to manifest the Holy Sword again with no success.

"■■■■...!"

Shardark slammed Veira into the ground and charged at the bone construct.

"Tsk—tenth-order spell, Meld Gaiez!"

Bwoooosh!

A pillar of white-hot flames erupted, burning through the night, but it did nothing to stop Shardark's advance.

That accursed monster!

Leonis raised his hand, and a moment later, chains shot out of the darkness, coiling around Shardark. This was one of the Arc Seven, a Dark-Lord-slaying weapon created by the gods—the Vile Dragon Fetter, Ragva Zol.

These chains had stopped Veira's rampage in the capital when she went berserk, and the Arc Seven were exceptionally potent against Dark Lords. Additionally, Ragva Zol had a curse that made it stronger against dragons.

The binds stopped Shardark's charge.

I knew it!

Shardark had fused with more than just a Dark Lord. As one of the Six Heroes, he was blessed by the Luminous Powers and had merged with countless forms of life to achieve continual evolution.

Naturally, he'd sought to acquire a dragon at some point. And as Shardark froze in place...

"*Graaaaaaaaaaaaaah!*"

...Veira fired a beam of argent heat at him, while Rivaiz cast a ninth-order ice spell from above, the Demon Frost Blizzard—Hield Berzed.

"Burst forth, darkness—Arzam!" Leonis followed up with a flurry of tenth-order spells.

Boom, boom, boom boom boom!

Destructive mana exploded, illuminating the world like a sun at noon.

◆

The many attacks from the trio of Dark Lords silenced the Void King. He stood amid roaring, crimson fire, his body grievously wounded.

Crack.

A fissure ran through space.

"...?!"

Crack, crack, crack...

The fractures expanded swiftly, swallowing up the nearby area in no time.

Leonis swallowed nervously. *Did we...do it...?*

They certainly hadn't dealt a fatal wound. The Void King wasn't going to perish from this. However, during the fight in the Seventh Assault Garden, Shardark retreated into a tear in reality after being shot by Leonis's Holy Sword.

Maybe he couldn't maintain his form after taking a certain degree of damage? Or perhaps there was a time limit to how long he could fight.

Crack...crack...crack...!

<God...apostle...■■■■...!> Shardark said something akin to words.

"Oh," Leonis said ironically, raising an eyebrow. "I'm surprised you can still speak, my teacher."

Crash, clink, crunch!

Shardark blew the chains of Ragva Zol away.

<*The goddess's apostles...must...be destroyed...*>

"What...? What are you saying?"

"Undead King, I'm preparing a powerful attack. Stall him for me," Rivaiz declared from above.

"Do you understand what you're asking of me?!" Leonis grumbled from atop the bone sculpture.

Rivaiz's water mantle shone, and a half-transparent sphere of water surrounded her body.

"■■■■■■■—!"

Shardark howled, swinging Ragva Zol around.

"...Tch!"

The chains bashed against the Skull Colossus, shattering its arm to bits.

The Skull Colossus is a siege weapon! How can it shatter it this easily?!

Having been knocked off the sculpture, Leonis reflexively cast a gravity spell to descend safely to the ground. Gigantic chunks of bone rained from above. He'd hoped the construct would provide a distraction while he fired his Holy Sword, but that plan failed.

If Leonis had had Blackas with him, he'd have been able to fight another way. There was also his third minion, still locked within the Realm of Shadows, although that was a perilous option.

I never counted on not being able to manifest my Holy Sword, though.

Leonis glanced at his right hand. He couldn't see the hex pattern, but it wasn't gone yet. Leonis was an expert when it came to curses, but this was no ordinary magic. He'd never seen a pattern like it before.

What a nuisance...

Clicking his tongue, Leonis bolted through the darkness. He didn't have to try to sense Shardark's presence, given that his giant form shook the ground with every step.

"The Evil-Rending Sword—Zolgstar Mezekis!" Leonis turned around and swung his arm, calling upon the Realm of Shadows.

Several dozen blades emerged from thin air, lancing toward Shardark. These were copies made from fragments of one of the Arc Seven. Their power was inferior to the original, but they were still effective against Dark Lords.

However...

Clangggg!

...Shardark swept away the flurry of blades with a single stroke of his broadsword. And then, much to Leonis's surprise, he caught a few of them to wield as his own.

No weaponry is effective against him...

Even after being reduced to a Void monstrosity, Shardark's authority as one of the Six Heroes, granted to him by the Luminous Powers, remained in effect. His ability to wield all armaments in the world extended even to the Arc Seven.

Blue fire billowed out of Shardark's sole eye, which remained fixed upon Leonis. He swung Zolgstar Mezekis's blades down on the boy. No spell could meet this attack.

"*Grahhhhhhhhhhhhh!*"

A massive red dragon closed its giant jaws on Shardark's arm, crushing it.

"Veira?!"

"Feel the vengeance of the Demon Dragon's Mountain Range's dragons!"

The mighty creature's claws, wreathed in flames, tore through the Void King's hardened skin. Black miasma gushed like blood.

Shardark swung down the Arc Seven swords, thrusting them into Veira's neck, but her dragon scales deflected them easily.

"You underestimate the Dragon Lord if you think you can harm me with imitations!" Veira roared, her tail flailing like a whip to strike at Shardark's body. The Swordmaster lost balance, his massive form crumpling to the ground. Seizing upon that chance...

"Hear my roar, fool—Dei Argh Dragray!"

...Veira sank her claws into Shardark, undoing his divine protection as she spoke a spell in the dragon tongue.

Bwoooooooooooooooosh!

Before Veira could attack again...

"*Grahhhhhhhh!*" she roared out in agony.

...Shardark's arm emerged from the fire, tearing off one of the Dragon Lord's wings. Shardark rose up and grabbed the dragon by one of its horns. He then used another arm to try driving a lance through her throat.

"Veira!" Leonis cried.

"That's long enough. Beware, Dragon Lord, you might get caught up in this," Leonis heard Rivaiz state.

"Hmph... You certainly took your time!"

Veira reverted to her humanoid form to escape the Swordmaster.

"Frozen souls, slumber in the eternal palace—Rei Zava Cocytus!"

A prismatic shining barrier of ice pushed against Shardark's gigantic form. Rivaiz invoked a powerful, highly advanced eleventh-order limit-break spell. This was magic unique to sea sprites. It allowed them to trap targets within an ice block formed of mana, forcing the captive into an eternal slumber.

Shardark's spell resistance was powerless in the face of this magic. The ice barrier held him in place.

However, the triumph was only momentary. Shardark's sole eye continued to burn and glow within the ice block's absolute zero environment. If the three Dark Lords didn't capitalize on this opening, they would lose their chance at striking down the Void King.

Leonis was already prepared to chant the spell. Veira had risked herself to give the time needed, and Rivaiz provided the moment to loose it. Leonis couldn't afford to let this opportunity go to waste.

He pointed the tip of the Staff of Sealed Sins at Shardark, focusing his mana into it.

—Hark the song of ruin. Ashes to ashes, dust to dust—

—The tragedy that returns all to its origin, once again, descends upon us solemnly—

Leonis hadn't chanted a limit-break spell—a spell of the eleventh order and above—since reincarnating. Spells of that level required longer chants, meaning there weren't many chances to use them in live combat. However, the greater reason he'd avoided casting one was the strain using so much mana would have on his current body.

No ordinary spell will work on him, though... Leonis gritted his teeth. Intense sparks flickered from the tip of the staff in his hands.

"Ngh... Ahhh...!"

The discharge of mana burned at his fingertips. Every nerve in his body screamed out in pain.

As I suspected, this form can't handle it...!

Slender fingers slid over Leonis's.

"Veira?!"

"I'll lend you my mana, Leo!" Veira said, standing behind him with a smile.

Leonis's mana circulated through Veira and then into his staff. The rod shone, overflowing with magical power.

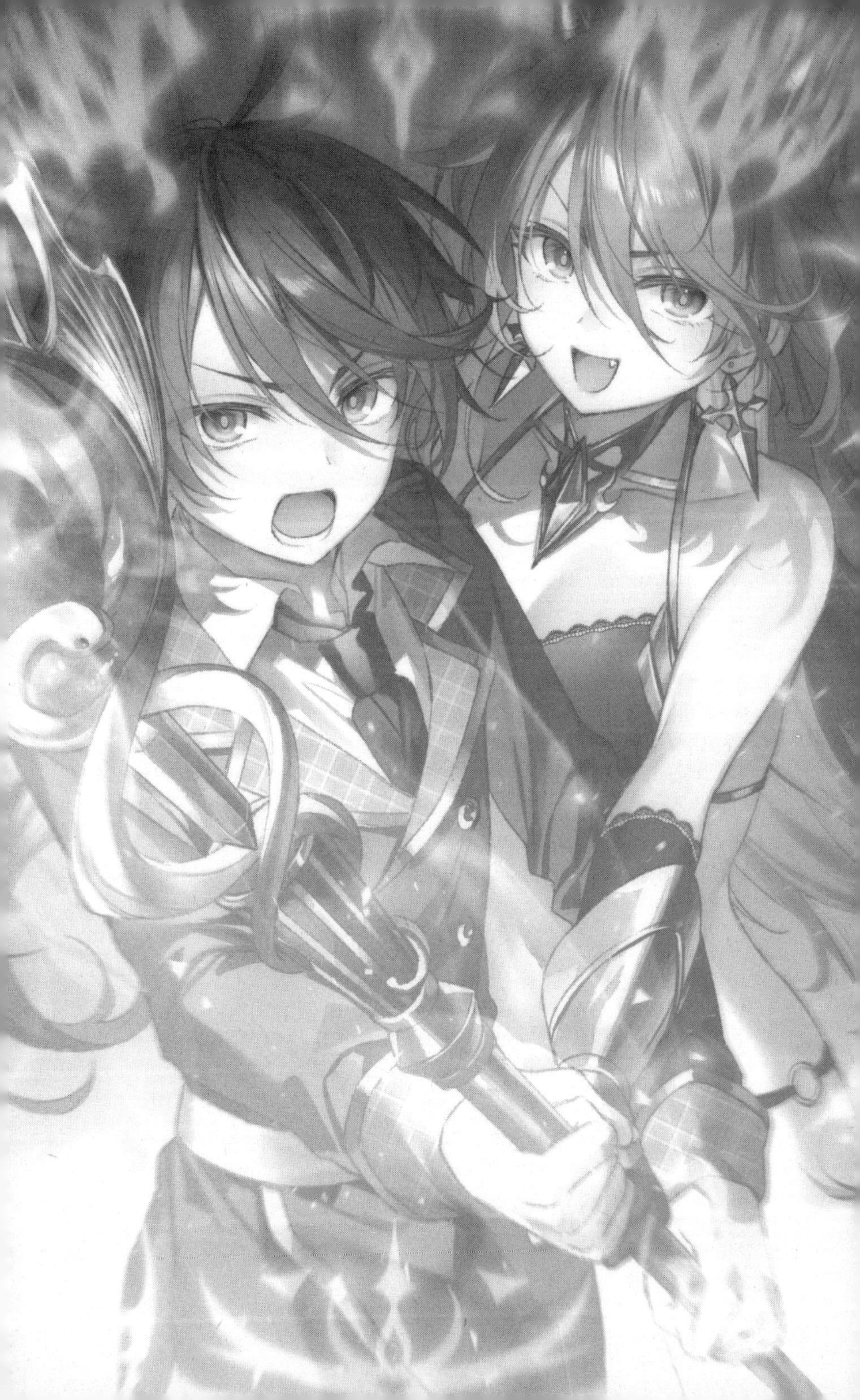

"May my rage burn the world away, hastening the time of ruin...!"

Just as the ice barrier encasing Shardark shattered...

"Eleventh-order destruction spell—Meld Magnus!"

Booooooooooooooom!

...destructive light covered the world. A swarm of Voids that emerged from a tear in space evaporated instantly. And...

Crack, crack, crack...

...the cracks around Shardark Void Lord multiplied.

"...Leo...nis..."

"...?!"

Within the surging red flames, the Void Lord...called his name.

"Are you...the...successor...?"

For a moment, Leonis thought he saw his teacher's eye regain the intellect it possessed when it still belonged to a hero. Shardark reached out, as though to grasp something, then vanished into a tear in space.

Crack, crack, crack...

The fracture that swallowed Shardark began to eat into the ground. It grew, threatening to swallow the sky. The world was breaking, transformed into a shattered palace of glass.

Leonis's eyes widened in alarm as he peered overhead.

...That's...! Could it be?!

"Leo, we have to run!"

"What are you dawdling for? At this rate, we'll be overtaken, too!"

Veira and Rivaiz both warned him, yet Leonis stayed put and spoke with conviction. "We should let it. It's probably..."

"Huh?! Leo!"

The canopy of the sky crumbled...and the world inverted.

◆

The surroundings changed immediately.

Leonis shook his head lightly and looked around. He wasn't in the crater where Ironblood Castle had stood, but in a forest full of dense trees. Sunlight was beginning to color the dim sky.

"...Where are we?" Veira whispered behind him. Turning around, Leonis saw the crimson-haired girl eyeing him with a confused expression. "Were we thrown to another world again?" she asked.

"...No. This is probably our original one," Leonis replied. "I saw the stars through the crack in space..."

"Stars?"

"Yes..." Leonis nodded and glanced up at the sky visible through the forest canopy.

The Star of Calamity shone ominously as the heavens grew bright. Entering that fracture in reality had been a gamble.

But we managed to find a way back.

They'd failed to pursue the Devil of the Underworld, but there was little alternative.

"Undead King, where did the Swordmaster disappear to?" Rivaiz descended from the air, her water mantle fluttering.

"If he's not here, then perhaps he used the tear to travel elsewhere," Leonis replied, shaking his head.

The Voids likely used those fractures to freely traverse dimensions, but if that was the case...it made no sense that they appeared and disappeared so irregularly, like fog. If the Voids could move so easily, humanity would have been driven to extinction by now.

"Why did the Swordmaster of the Six Heroes... Why did he appear there?"

"...Good question. I don't know."

Shardark had definitely reacted to the goddess's voice, but what he'd come there to do was unclear. Maybe he'd long since lost all sense of purpose and had gone mad from the emptiness eating away at his soul, and so he'd been drawn to this remnant of his old nemesis.

"What was that world...?" Rivaiz muttered.

A red sky. A wasteland that expanded endlessly. Swarms of countless Voids. Leonis speculated that world was the source of the Voids, but what were the ruins of the Lord of Beasts' citadel doing there? And why did he hear the voice of the deceased goddess...?

Leonis reflexively gripped the Staff of Sealed Sins. The Devil of the Underworld and Duke Crystalia. The Azure Hold. The Void world. The goddess's voice. The Ironblood Castle ruins that shouldn't have been there.

Something connected all these pieces.

Azra-Ael must have the answer.

For now, Leonis was back in his world, and another matter demanded his attention.

I can't leave my kingdom unattended for long.

It wouldn't do to leave Blackas and Shary in charge of everything. Leonis thought of his minion. It had been only a few days, yet he felt oddly wistful.

I did promise, after all.

Leonis retrieved his terminal from his pocket.

"All right. Where are we?"

He tried activating the device, but it didn't provide any information on the surrounding area. The magical apparatuses of this era weren't of much use unless they were within range of an Assault Garden.

"If you're looking for a human city, you'll find one that way," Veira said, pointing toward the dawn.

"Are you certain?" Leonis asked.

"Of course I am," the Dragon Lord replied, grinning and placing her hands on her waist. "Dragons fly by watching the positions of the stars."

"How far is it?"

"Well, I don't know that much."

"I see." Leonis nodded. "Then I must return to the capital. I'm wary of Azra-Ael's plans, but I have a promise to keep."

"Hmm. I bet that minion of yours is worried about you," Veira teased.

"I will go after the Devil of the Underworld," Rivaiz decided. "I must reclaim my leviathan."

"Me too. He still has the Azure Hold... Though for all we know, Azra-Ael and the Azure Hold aren't in this world at all," Veira remarked.

"If his objective is to collect the Dark Lords, he will have to return. Knowing as much, we should inspect the lands where the remaining Dark Lords slumber."

"True."

"You're right. I will seek the Lord of Beasts' resting place."

"Okay. Let us know if you find anything."

Leonis summoned his skull dragon from the Realm of Shadows and hopped onto its back. "Don't be careless. There's no telling what Azra-Ael might be planning," he warned the other two.

"Hmph. I'll reduce him to ashes next time," Veira declared.

The skull dragon flapped its wings and took off toward the sun.

◆

It was evening. Having finished her exercises for the day, Riselia returned to her room in the hotel, where she changed out of her training outfit and into her underwear. She collapsed on the sofa.

"I...I think...I'm done for..."

She whined most uncharacteristically, her hair disheveled. Normally, Riselia wouldn't act so undisciplined, even with no one watching. But she was utterly exhausted from multiple days of rigorous training.

On top of the eighteenth platoon's team practice sessions, which Riselia herself had scheduled, she also had to spend every morning and evening suffering through special lessons. Worse yet, her instructor was quite unforgiving.

Riselia had improved at handling the True Ancestor's Dress and controlling her mana circulation, but she couldn't say by how much or if it would matter.

Lying atop the sofa, Riselia fidgeted in place uneasily, turning around to look up at the mana lamp lighting the room.

"When's Leo coming back...?" she muttered.

Four days had passed since he left the capital. She'd messaged him on each one but never received a reply. Riselia kept a cup of pudding in the fridge, waiting for him in case he returned.

"Leo..."

Riselia played with the sofa's buttons, pushing them in. She grabbed a cushion she used as a pillow and sank her fangs into it.

With puffed-up cheeks, she decided, "Not good enough."

Riselia was frustrated. She tossed and turned on the sofa, still hugging the cushion. Eventually, her eyes settled on the half-open window. The curtain danced from the soft breeze. Outside, the sun was sinking, and the casino's neon lights were sparking to life.

The girl stared vacantly at the fluttering curtain. He'd been gone for only a few days, but she missed him desperately...

Once Leo comes back, I'm going to suck a whole lot of blood from him.

Riselia hugged the cushion tightly. Her mana sizzled, making her heart throb.

Ba-dump. Ba-dump. Ba-dump.

Huh? I-I'm feeling, kind of... Huh? Thinking about him made her cheeks flush. *N-no...Leo is, well, he's ten years old... That's not...*

Riselia's heart beat like a drum, and she felt her face grow hot.

"...!"

The doorknob clicked.

"Leo?!" Riselia sat up at once.

"Sorry, I'm not the kid. It's your favorite maid, Lady Selia. ♪"

The door opened, revealing Regina in a maid's uniform. She struck a strange, cute pose, her twintails bobbing.

"...Oh. It's just you, Regina." Riselia's shoulders slumped in plain disappointment.

"You know, Lady Selia, that reaction kind of breaks my heart," Regina muttered dispassionately.

"Ah, n-no, I'm sorry! I'm glad you're here, Regina!"

The maid shrugged. "Hmm. Fine, I'll forgive you. Anyway, it's time for the meeting."

"Oh, right. I'll go prepare."

Riselia got off the sofa and hurriedly changed into her uniform. As she put on her skirt, she looked out the window again. No one was there, of course. There was only the gently billowing curtain.

Leo...

◆

A petite shadow stood atop the Shangri-la Resort's rooftop. Shary had dropped her Leonis disguise and was in her usual maid's attire.

"My lord..."

Her hands were together, as though in prayer, while she watched the setting sun. Whenever Leonis went out to battle, Shary waited on Death Hold's balcony to wish for her master's safety.

She was confident of his victory, but that didn't mean she wasn't concerned. After all, at present, her master was in the vessel of a child.

And his opponent this time is the Lord of the Seas, touted as the strongest Dark Lord...

Even with all her faith in Leonis and his powers, Shary couldn't help but wonder if he would return unscathed this time.

"Are you worried for Lord Magnus?" a calm voice inquired.

Shary turned around, her gaze settling on a black wolf with golden eyes, standing in the shadow of the setting sun.

"Lord Blackas..."

Blackas stood alongside Shary, turning his eyes to the horizon.

"My friend is sure to return to his kingdom. All we can do is believe in him," he said.

"Yes, you're right..." Shary bowed her head reverently.

"Incidentally, Shary, should Lord Magnus be late for the Holy Sword Dance Festival, it will fall to you to attend as his body double."

She nodded. "I've made the necessary preparations."

Shary had studied the rules thoroughly in preparation. A human combat festival was child's play to one with the skills of a Septentrion assassin. She could win in a manner that wasn't too spectacular or lose in a way that wasn't too crushing.

The girl didn't intend to throw the match, but she wasn't planning on actively fighting. A needless show of her strength would attract undue attention to Leonis.

"I hope nothing happens, but the trifling fools who get in Lord Magnus's way time and again might take advantage of the celebration. Bear that in mind."

"Yes, understood."

The Voids weren't the only mysterious faction in this world. Past officers of the Dark Lords' Armies, like Nefakess and Zemein, had reappeared in this era, and conspired against Leonis. Shary herself had been attacked and suffered an embarrassing defeat at the hands of one of their demonic assassins.

I won't let it happen again...

With resolve in heart, Shary touched the ring in her pocket.

Leonis had given it to her. It was capable of summoning the strongest being in the Dark Lords' Armies. She'd used it once already, so the magic had faded, but it was still a dear treasure.

My lord, please... Be safe, Shary prayed, her eyes fixed on the horizon.

◆

The days in Camelot came and went. The special training intensified as the Holy Sword Dance Festival approached. Fortunately, everyone showed clear signs of improving and maturing.

Before long, the day of the event arrived.

CHAPTER 8

THE HOLY SWORD DANCE FESTIVAL

It was 10:30 Imperial Standard Time—the day of the Holy Sword Dance Festival.

The members of the eighteenth platoon boarded a large, self-driving vehicle that transported them to the stage of the festival in the Eighth Assault Garden.

Since the Eighth Assault Garden was still under construction, its surface area was only a third of the Seventh Assault Garden's. It had two cutting-edge mana furnaces as its energy source, and upon completion, it was set to boast the highest mobility of all its kind.

"Construction is currently at seventy-eight percent, but since they'll need to divert resources to repairing the Seventh Assault Garden, it'll take two more years for it to be completed," Elfiné said from the seat opposite Riselia's.

"It already looks pretty much done, though," Regina noted as she looked out the window.

The vehicle was driving through Area III, passing by many large buildings. They were all deserted, and it reminded Riselia of the Third Assault Garden.

Despite this being an unpopulated city, destroying any structures outside the designated combat area would mean a loss of points. This rule put Regina at a disadvantage, since her Holy Sword's Drag Blast attack was a wide-area bombardment, but the regulations were based on real urban combat, so there was nothing to be done.

"Where are we headed?" Riselia asked.

"It's pretty far from the Central Garden," Elfiné replied, tapping her terminal.

Each unit participating in the Holy Sword Dance Festival had a designated starting spot. These positions were kept secret from the participants. Each site in a team's area had core flags in place, and by stealing them, a rival unit would score points, and the defending one would lose points.

A team member was disqualified when knocked unconscious or if their Holy Sword was destroyed. Baiting enemies out using the core flags would be a helpful strategy.

The game area appeared to be vast and included underground passages. However, as time passed, float blocks would be detached from the game area, and partitions would descend to seal off underground passages. The constantly shrinking game area would force a conflict even if a team tried to run around with a core flag and remain elusive.

The vehicle drove past the urban area and got on a highway. Riselia looked up at the blue sky.

Leo...

He hadn't made it back in time. The one seated next to her right now was his body double.

"You want a sweet, kid?" Sakuya asked.

"Yes, please."

Sakuya pulled a castella from her sleeve, which the body double gladly accepted.

Is the faker worried about Leo, too? Riselia wondered. "Miss Finé, has the broadcast started already?" she asked.

"Yes, there are drones scattered around the city."

The machines were controlled by Artificial Elementals, which used the Astral Garden to transmit what each team was doing to large screens in each Assault Garden.

The vehicle continued out of the urban area and entered an underground tunnel. Finally it came to a stop before a gigantic supply silo, and a voice played from inside the vehicle.

"Arrived at Point E. Members of the eighteenth platoon are to stay put until they receive the signal marking the opening of the Holy Sword Dance Festival."

◆

"Hmm... The seats for invited guests should be around here..." Arle turned her head this way and that. She had the ticket Sakuya gave her clutched in one hand.

She was in a spectator stadium set up on Excalibur Academy's premises. The arena was open to all citizens. The large screens used for student matches would instead show the festival activities. There weren't usually many spectators here, but the Holy Sword Dance Festival had brought people out in droves.

This place is even more crowded than the Rognas Kingdom's marketplace. It's making me dizzy.

Arle was bad with crowds and longed for the sacred tranquility of the Spirit Forest. Honestly, she wanted to leave but refused to let Sakuya's ticket go to waste.

Besides, I would like to see how the strongest warriors of this era fight...

It took a while, but Arle finally found a seat. Yet just as she went to sit, she spotted a familiar child a few rows ahead.

Is that Tessera? What is she doing here...?

The young girl was from an orphanage Arle had eaten at once. She was walking along a passage in front of the many rows of chairs, unsure where to go.

"You there, girl."

Tessera turned around, surprised. "Miss Arle...?" Her eyes widened upon seeing a familiar face. Arle motioned for Tessera to approach, and she did. "Hello," she greeted her with a polite bow of her head. "Did you come to watch the festival, too, Miss Arle?"

"...I suppose. I am curious about this," Arle replied, using a finger to play with her ponytail. "Is that why you're here?"

"Yes. Big Sis Riselia gave me a ticket, but I can't find my seat..." Tessera retrieved her ticket from a pocket, showing it to Arle.

"Let me have a look. I can help with your search." Arle inspected the printed number. "Hmm... Isn't this...? Yes, it's the chair next to mine."

"I-it is?"

Sakuya was in the same unit as that Riselia girl, so it followed they'd received tickets for adjacent spots. Arle and Tessera bought popcorn and drinks from a passing trolley and settled in.

"Did you come here alone? No one's watching you?"

"No, I'm here by myself. I come to watch the matches here all the time."

"I see..."

A thousand years ago, even in relatively peaceful countries like the Rognas Kingdom, abductors wandered the outskirts of the cities. A girl walking about unsupervised was unthinkable. However, things were different in the Seventh Assault Garden, and this was Excalibur Academy, likely the safest place in the city.

Although technically, I am in a criminal organization.

Remembering that made Arle gloomy. She'd joined to learn the Dark Lord Zol Vadis's identity, but she'd since become the Demon Wolf Pack's designated bodyguard.

The screen displayed each school's representatives.

How does this work, exactly? Do they use spirits or familiars to project this image through some kind of Farsight sorcery?

It boggled Arle's mind to consider how developed present-day magical apparatuses were.

Why were the ancient ways of sorcery discarded, and how did all of this technology advance?

While she thought on it...

"H-hey, what's that?"

"I—I don't know. How did it get in here...?"

...Arle heard a minor commotion from the seats behind her. Upon turning around, she saw...

"What? A-a dog?!" Arle nearly dropped her popcorn.

...a large hound with pitch-black fur walking among the stands. It carried itself with the gait of a king, as though expecting all others to vacate its path.

Arle frowned suspiciously. *Why is there a dog here?*

"Ah, Fluffymaru!" Tessera got up and waved to the beast.

"...Fluffy?" Arle repeated, confused.

The dog noticed Tessera and approached. It obediently took a spot next to the girl.

"Did you come to watch like we did, Fluffymaru?" she asked.

"*Woof...,*" the great hound barked.

"You know this dog?" Arle questioned.

Tessera nodded while rubbing under Fluffymaru's chin. "Yes. He comes to the orphanage sometimes to play."

"I...see..." Arle gazed at Fluffymaru.

She liked animals, as all elves did, yet an instinct told her to remain on guard around this black dog. He reminded her too much of another... The Black Wolf Emperor, who was the Undead King's trusted companion. Blackas Shadow Prince struck terror in the kingdom's army with his jaws of death.

Of course, this couldn't possibly be him... But that dark fur, creeping night given form, and those golden eyes... Arle couldn't help but think of that fearsome demon.

"D-does he bite?" Arle asked cautiously.

"Don't be afraid. Fluffymaru is a good boy," Tessera replied, still scratching the animal's chin. It closed its eyes in satisfaction.

R-right. Blindly fearing this hound wouldn't do.

Arle calmed herself and returned her attention to the large screen. No sooner had she done so than a familiar face appeared.

"Ah, it's Big Sis Riselia!" Tessera leaned forward and pointed.

The screen showed portrait shots of each member of the eighteenth platoon, the characteristics of their respective Holy Swords, and graphs detailing statistics calculated from practice matches.

"Now then," a commentator's voice boomed. **"This is a group that's drawn a lot of attention. It's Excalibur Academy's special entry squad. Riselia Crystalia, the leader of the eighteenth platoon and my eternal rival, is on the screen right now. Why, I recall our first meeting. It was some ten years ago, when I was pursuing a giant lizard that escaped one of Duke Crystalia's parties—"**

"Er, Miss Fenris, please keep your commentary impartial."

"What are you saying, President?! I haven't even begun my stor—mmmg!"

"My apologies for this shameful broadcast, good listeners."

After a bit of static, the commentary ended.

The stadium's spectators were all riled up by the introduction of Excalibur Academy's representatives.

"Look, look! That boy is so cute. ♪ How old is he?"

"He's only ten. If we just let him sit for a few more years...he might be ripe for the picking."

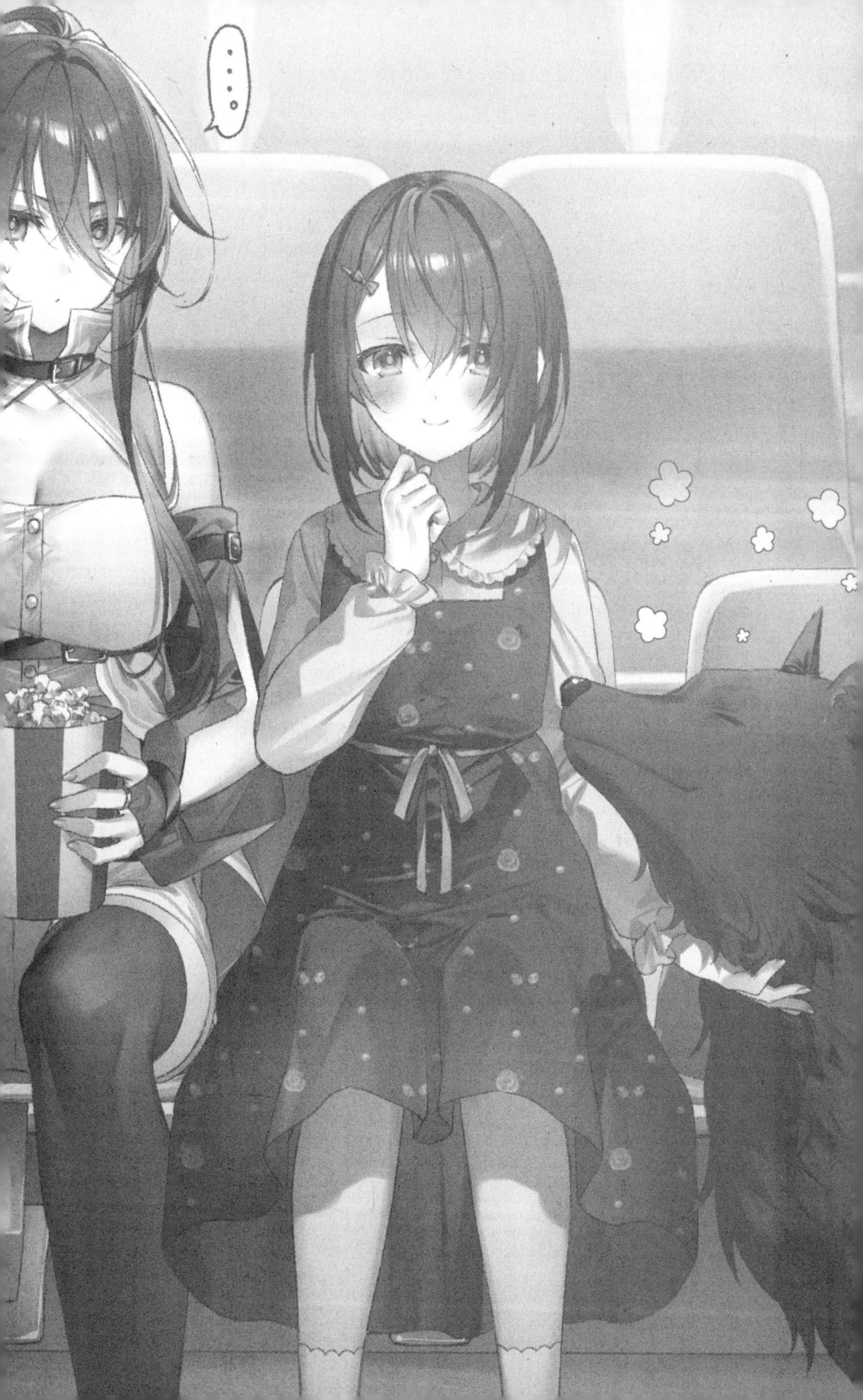

....

"Cute boys like that grow up to be Dark Lords in the bedroom."

Arle overheard some nearby girls wearing Excalibur Academy uniforms discussing a boy who'd come on-screen. It seemed he was rather popular among...

"Leo..."

Arle glanced at Tessera, who gazed at the screen with rosy cheeks.

Oh my. She's a precocious one, isn't she? Arle chuckled.

A girl in love. Arle envied Tessera a little. Having been raised as a hero since infancy, she had never been allowed to experience romance. Arle's thoughts drifted to her past, one thousand years ago. The visage of her fellow apprentice, who'd studied under the same master as her, came to mind. She'd always admired him for working so hard to save the world.

Perhaps...he was my first love.

Yet the hero she'd once admired had gone on to become a Dark Lord who threatened humanity.

Wh-what am I thinking?! I can't believe myself...

The elf girl shook her head vigorously and focused her attention on the screen.

◆

The Imperial Standard Time was 10:40.

Sitting beneath the glow of the underground silo's mana lamps, Riselia and her platoon awaited the signal for the match to start. Riselia and Elfiné were huddled around their terminals, discussing strategy. Regina was leaning on a wall doing stretches, while Sakuya munched on a famous Sakura Orchid food called a sushi roll. Shary, disguised as Leonis, snuck longing glances at Sakuya's snack.

"Starting underground is kind of an advantage. The other teams are gonna have a harder time finding us," Regina said.

Riselia shook her head calmly. "Not necessarily. If we had a locational advantage, you'd be right, but an Assault Garden's underground passages are long and winding. Fighting down here will demand different tactics than if we were aboveground."

They'd have to analyze countless underground routes to guess at what opposing squads might do. Compared to the surface, where large fights would break out almost as soon as the match began, this station would require the eighteenth platoon to deploy members more cautiously.

"Also, anywhere below the fourth underground level is considered off-limits," Elfiné cautioned while showing everyone the map on her terminal. "The linear rail tracks are down there, and they don't want us to damage them."

The Holy Sword Dance Festival allowed participants to bring their terminals, but their communication features were limited outside specific areas. This was meant to mimic the kind of EMP (Excessive Mana Pulse) jamming they might encounter in real combat against the Voids.

Regina tapped her chin with a finger. "I wonder which other groups are nearby."

"I think we can rule out the other Excalibur Academy representatives," Riselia replied. "And Princess Chatres's unit is likely on the surface, so we won't run into them soon."

Highly rated units were set on the surface so they would clash early on and get the audience excited. From the higher-ups' perspective, it was foolish to put the winning team—Chatres's in particular—underground. The princess was too popular and charismatic.

"I mentioned it during this morning's meeting, but," Elfiné

said in a hushed-up voice, wary of the surveillance drones, "we should probably be careful of the Fourth Assault Garden's Academia unit."

The Academia was an institute primarily for Holy Sword researchers, and its teams rarely scored highly at the Holy Sword Dance Festival. Its top-ranked students were very capable, but they didn't draw the same attention as the large-scale Excalibur Academy or the elite students of Halcyon Academy.

However, Count Deinfraude Phillet governed the Fourth Assault Garden, and Finzel Phillet was an Academia alumnus.

"It's possible research for the Demon Sword Project was conducted at the Academia. I doubt they'll try to do something during an event as major as the Holy Sword Dance Festival, but we should keep that in mind."

There was a minute left until the match began. Riselia got to her feet, her expression serious. Shary, naturally still disguised as Leonis, took her sleeve.

"Miss Selia."

"...What's wrong, Leo? Do you want a sweet?"

"No," Shary replied, exasperated. "I've already told you this, but remember that I will only be able to offer minimal support."

Riselia nodded. "That's fine. I'll show you how much stronger I am from all that training."

"I see." Shary averted her gaze. "If nothing else, I will admit you have guts. You worked very hard."

"Th-thanks." Riselia smiled sheepishly.

At 11:00 Imperial Standard Time, the horn signaling the start of the Holy Sword Dance Festival echoed over the Eighth Assault Garden.

""""Holy Sword—Activate!""""

The members of the eighteenth platoon all spoke the words as one, manifesting their Holy Swords. Regina's Drag Striker,

Sakuya's Raikirimaru, Elfiné's Eye of the Witch, and Riselia's Bloody Sword. "Leonis" likewise conjured the replica of the Staff of Sealed Sins, which was registered as his Holy Sword.

What made this event different from the usual interschool bouts was the ability to disqualify an opponent by destroying their Holy Sword. Once a Holy Sword was broken, it was forbidden for its wielder to call it back. Additionally, all competitors had to have their Holy Swords manifested constantly.

Riselia glanced at Regina, Elfiné, and Leonis as she spoke. "As previously discussed, we'll head out to claim core flags." Once the three of them nodded, Riselia's eyes went to Sakuya. "We're counting on you."

"Yes, understood. I'll do my best to keep moving." Sakuya brandished Raikirimaru lightly.

Sakuya's role was to go up to the surface alone and scout enemy teams. If possible, she would use hit-and-run tactics to keep opponents distracted. Essentially, she was a hyper-offensive decoy. Having the strongest member of the eighteenth platoon operating solo would hopefully disrupt the opposing squads. This kind of tactic was only possible thanks to Sakuya's overwhelming skills and Raikirimaru's powers over acceleration.

"Don't blame me if I sweep the whole match, though," Sakuya boasted.

"Be careful not to get too involved in any fights. Your main role is to scout and cause disarray," Riselia reminded her with a strained smile. "All right. Let's go!" Riselia raised her voice dignifiedly, the Bloody Sword in her hand.

◆

At the same time...

Elysion Academy's first platoon members, led by Chatres Ray

O'ltriese, activated their Holy Swords. They stood at the heart of the Central Garden.

"As expected, everyone's eyes are on the princess," a young man shouldering a hunting gun–type Holy Sword remarked flippantly. "I'm sure they're getting lots of flattering pictures of you, Silver-Blooded Sword Princess."

Three drones buzzed around the area.

"We don't have time for chatter, Colt." Chatres glared at the young man coldly, and he went silent immediately.

As frivolous as Colt appeared, he was a first-rate sniper. Unsurprisingly, each member of Chatres's squad was a skilled elite, fully devoted and obedient to the princess. They were disciplined and moved with precision according to her orders.

That Chatres could skillfully unite and command a group of idiosyncratic talents was due to more than her royal status. It was because all her teammates recognized her overwhelming prowess. The members of Chatres's platoon were her faithful pawns on the battlefield.

A commander couldn't have asked for better fighters. However, that meant the blame for a loss all fell upon Chatres. She had long since accepted that intense pressure, though.

The three royal houses were meant to serve as a banner for humanity to unite under in the war against the Voids. If Chatres couldn't handle this challenge, then she had no place among royalty.

"Ah, I've detected something. Some bugs hiding in a large building in Area IV," a girl reported in a carefree tone. She was holding a terminal and used a scanner-type Holy Sword.

"Which unit are they from?"

"The St. Eluminas Monastery's fourth choir. Their Holy Swords' abilities are—"

"It's fine, I know all their abilities," Chatres cut in, shaking her head.

"Running into us right away is pretty bad luck for them," a tall man with a stern expression remarked. He was from a family line that served House O'ltriese. "Should I use my Holy Sword to level the enemy base, Your Highness?"

"No, I'll do it. The audience needs a demonstration."

To Chatres, winning the Holy Sword Dance Festival was a matter of duty. And victory alone wasn't enough. She needed to show off her incredible power and crush all opponents directly. Doing so would boost the royal family's authority and better secure its status as the guardian and hope of the entire human race.

Chatres drew her Holy Sword in a fluid motion, letting the silver broadsword reflect the sunlight. "Holy Sword—Ragna Nova." She held the weapon up and then swung it down at once. A flash of light ran across the sky for a moment.

Boooooooooom!

Far in the distance, a building was severed in half, its top section collapsing and crashing to the ground.

"Princess, they might scold us if you go too hard," Colt whispered, looking exasperated.

"I made sure it wasn't a direct blow. No one participating would be foolish enough to get caught and die in an attack like that." Chatres lowered her shining sword.

"No, er, I mean we'll lose points for destroying buildings..."

"It doesn't matter. A single core flag will negate that."

The princess had destroyed the building to demonstrate her might to the audience. The Holy Sword Dance Festival's organizers wanted Chatres to put on a spectacle.

"Now, the hunt is on. And our target"—Chatres looked up at the clear sky—"is the leader of Excalibur Academy's eighteenth platoon, Riselia Crystalia."

CHAPTER 9

VOID SHIFT

Multiple sets of footfalls echoed through the abandoned underground tunnel. Riselia and her group moved as a straight line, racing through the labyrinthine channels. Two Eye of the Witch orbs floated ahead of them, lighting the way. The spheres guided the group along, probed for enemies, and scanned for traps all at once.

This had initially been a simple, straightforward tunnel for transporting supplies, but with partitions closing different parts of the place, it became part of a maze.

"Everyone, stop," Elfiné warned. "There's a core flag reaction in a hundred-melte radius of us."

Core flags transmitted a faint mana pattern, allowing scanner-type Holy Swords to detect them and probe after their general direction.

"It's not moving, so I don't think any unit has claimed it yet."

"Seems like it's fairly close, but because of the winding tunnels and closing barriers, it might take a while to get there. Do you know which level it's on, Miss Finé?"

"It's above us... Probably the second one."

Riselia's group was currently on the fourth underground tier. A partition had already sealed off the nearest staircase, so they had to wander and find another way up.

It's possible another group might beat us to the punch... Riselia hummed with concern as she examined the map displayed on her terminal. Unfortunately, it didn't denote which partitions had closed.

"There's an elevator ahead." Regina pointed at a metallic door ahead of them. It looked like the industrial sort meant for transporting supplies.

"Is it usable?"

"The mana lights in this passage are on, so unless the higher-ups turned it off, it should be," Elfiné replied. She approached the control panel with an Eye of the Witch orb in tow. Smirking, she added, "Or I could just take control of it."

"I-I'd expect nothing less from you, Miss Finé," Riselia said, a strained smile on her lips.

"...Huh?" Elfiné's fingers froze, hovering before the panel.

"What's wrong?"

"This elevator, it's moving. Descending, I think."

"...?!"

Riselia raised her Holy Sword, stepped back, and waited on guard. A few seconds later, the door opened with a whir.

"Huh?"

Inside was a large, metallic hermit crab.

"Is that a Void Simulator?!"

These multilegged armored weapons were employed in training exercises. This one's large eye glowed red as it lunged forward for Riselia.

"...?!"

Screeeeeeeech!

Riselia reflexively blocked it with her Holy Sword's blade, but she was unable to curb the momentum, which sent her flying back.

...Wh-what?!

The members of the eighteenth platoon had heard that several dozen new Void Simulator models would be deployed as obstacles at the Holy Sword Dance Festival.

I didn't think it'd use an elevator to launch a preemptive attack on us!

"Leave Lady Selia alone!" Regina fired her Drag Striker.

Unfortunately, the bullets bounced off the Void Simulator's metallic body, producing sparks. The Drag Striker lacked the firepower to penetrate its reinforced Metahalcum plating. This training machine was meant for academy students, but it could be loaded with large artillery to provide covering fire for Holy Swordsmen during actual Void attacks. It was a powerful weapon in its own right.

The Void Simulator swung down one of its large front legs. Riselia kicked off the ground, evading it, and the leg sank into the ground with a thud, blowing a large hole into the concrete.

"Miss Finé, can you try hacking the Voids Simulator's Artificial Elemental...?!" Riselia asked.

"Yes, I'll try!"

"Whoops, can't let you do that!" a voice suddenly called out.

Riselia looked up in alarm. A boy with a small build was clinging to a duct in the ceiling. He threw something resembling a net down at Riselia and the others.

"Ahhh!" Elfiné got tangled, which rendered her immobile.

"Miss Finé?!" Riselia called out.

"Heh-heh, that's my Holy Sword, the Predator's Web. It's a living net, so you can forget escaping."

Riselia glared at the boy. "That uniform. You're from the Military Instruction School."

The Military Instruction School was the Second Assault

Garden's Holy Swordsmen training facility. It was the successor to the knight academy of the old empire and had been established before Excalibur Academy.

"Lucky me, I get to chew up a platoon of dropouts as soon as the match begins!" The boy smirked.

"Looks like he set up this trap...," Riselia whispered.

"That's right," a mechanical voice replied mockingly from within the Void Simulator.

"There must be another with a Holy Sword that can manipulate magical apparatuses and control them from afar," Elfiné said, still tangled in the net.

"A platoon of dropouts? Don't underestimate us!" Regina fired her Drag Striker.

"Whoa there." The boy nimbly took cover behind the duct. "My Holy Sword is strong enough to pin down Voids. Once you're caught, there's no escape."

The boy cast another Predator's Web in Regina's direction.

"Ahhhh!"

"Regina!" Riselia cried.

Regina fired, but the shots from her Drag Striker were caught in the net. She was snared...as was Leonis, who'd been standing by the maid.

"Oh, shoot, I got caught...," Leonis remarked in a very monotone voice as he thrashed in the bindings.

"Huh?! Leo?!" Riselia exclaimed despite herself.

Shary had definitely gotten caught on purpose.

Ngh. She did say she wouldn't help, but...

Leonis had kept hidden so far, so as not to draw attention, and the enemy Holy Swordsmen seemed not to notice him. It seemed likely that his body double was someone who was skilled at stealth.

I get the feeling the real Leo would've helped a bit more, Riselia thought as she leaped away.

She crouched to evade the Void Simulator's attack, then jumped to Elfiné's side. The Eye of the Witch could mode-shift into an offensive form, the Vorpal Ray, and launch powerful attacks over a large area. However, Elfiné was too tangled to concentrate enough for that.

If I cut the web...!

"Hah, you're next, Crystalia the dropout!"

Another net spread wide as it flew toward Riselia from above, but she brandished her Holy Sword.

Whish, whish, whish...!

The Bloody Sword unleashed multiple blades of blood, which cut the net to bits in the blink of an eye.

"What?!" the boy exclaimed in disbelief.

"That won't work on me!"

Riselia hurried to help Elfiné, with the dancing crimson razors following after.

"Whoa there, I can't let you do that!" a loud voice echoed through the underground passage.

Something flew at Riselia from the dark.

"...?!" Riselia reflexively hopped to the side, and an object sped past her cheek.

Boom!

A concrete wall behind the young woman shattered.

Another one?

Riselia peered into the darkness with her vampire's eyes. She spied the silhouette of a large-built man approaching her calmly.

"Oh-ho. You actually dodged it. Not bad for a unit of dropouts."

The figure stepped into view—a giant of a man carrying a chain.

"The Serpent Wielder, Kaiser Bouffolop," Riselia muttered.

Kaiser Boufflop was the ace attacker of the Military Instruction School. His Holy Sword, the Crush Vise, could move independently and smash Voids with its bite.

The Void Simulator and the nets were meant to stall and inhibit. Kaiser was the one who'd finish the job.

"Let me have some fun before I beat Chatres, okay?" Kaiser raised his burly arms.

His chain Holy Sword swung through the air and then returned to his hand. Great metallic jaws dangled at the end of the links, lined with jagged teeth.

"Hrahhhhh!" Kaiser swung his Holy Sword overhead and hurled the jaws forward.

Riselia dodged adroitly, but...

"...?!"

...the chain altered its trajectory in midair. It came snapping at Riselia from behind with movements that defied physics.

A partially autonomous Holy Sword that attacks its target regardless of its wielder's input...!

Riselia twisted to guard with the Blood Sword, yet the chain coiled around the weapon to yank it away.

"Ahh!" Riselia refused to release the Blood Sword, though. "Dance, my blade! Bloody Slash!"

Her Holy Sword shone, sending crimson blades at the chain, hammering it until it came free. Riselia got to her feet swiftly and fixed her stance.

"Ha-ha-ha! Not bad, Crystalia girl!" Kaiser pulled the Crush Vise back. Its snakelike jaws rose to rush at Riselia again.

The bloody razors dancing around the girl converged in one place to form a shield, but the Crush Vise burst through effortlessly. Riselia had no choice but to fall back. Giving up that much space would put her at a disadvantage, but without any chance to move in closer, she had to play defensively.

"Ha-ha-ha! What's wrong, girl? Eh?!"

Bang, bang, bang, baaaaaaang!

The chain changed its trajectory irregularly, digging into the underground passage's walls.

"Quit all that running! I'll lose points if I trash this place too hard!"

Bang, bang, thud!

Kaiser's wild swinging wound up sweeping the Void Simulator.

If this continues, he'll corner me before long!

Riselia steeled her nerves, gathered mana in her legs, and kicked off a nearby wall.

"...What?!"

She sprinted across the wall, launching a surprise attack at Kaiser Bouffolop!

"Whoops, can't let that fly."

"...?!"

The boy hiding in the duct launched a net at Riselia. Blood blades tore through the thing easily, but part of it still caught the young woman's legs, disrupting her flow of mana and knocking her off-balance. Although she managed to keep from collapsing to the ground...

"Take this!"

...Kaiser seized upon the momentary faltering, flinging the Crush Vise at Riselia. She managed to block it with her Holy Sword but couldn't offset the force of the collision, which sent her sailing backward.

"Selia!"

"Lady Selia!"

Regina and Elfiné both cried out for their friend.

"Khh... Ahhh!"

Riselia's body struck the floor hard. The impact send a terrible shudder through her bones, which left them feeling out of place.

"Ngh!"

Ignoring the pain as best she could, Riselia pushed off a knee and stood, the Bloody Sword in hand.

Why...? I'm using mana... Why does my body feel so heavy...?

Suddenly, she realized the answer.

Ah...

Riselia spun around, locking eyes with Leonis, who was still entangled in a net.

"Leo!" she called out to him. The boy answered only with a questioning look. "Can I *take them off* now?"

"...?" Leonis's expression betrayed his confusion. His eyes widened in realization after a moment, and he nodded while giving a thumbs-up.

"Huh? What are you talking about?" Kaiser asked, still brandishing the Crush Vise.

"I had them on even when I went to sleep, so I completely forgot about them."

Riselia focused mana in her limbs and then released it in a single burst. The darkness around her arms and legs came apart and fell into her shadow.

"Huh...? What did you just...?"

"Wow," Riselia whispered, her eyes wide with disbelief as she hopped in place several times. "I can't believe this. I feel so...light..."

"Hah! I don't know what you're mumbling about, but this is over!" Kaiser snapped the Crush Vise at her, hoping to deliver the final blow.

Before his attack connected, however, Riselia disappeared.

"What?"

The only sound was a gentle breeze.

"Behind you."

"...?!"

A flash of silver hair fluttered behind Kaiser.

"I'll beat you with the back of my blade," Riselia said.

"Ah...gah!"

The stroke of a sword knocked the Military Instruction School's ace out, and the Crush Vise vanished. A moment later, something dropped from the duct overhead, hitting the ground with a thud. The net-casting Holy Swordsman lay on the ground, his eyes devoid of expression.

◆

"They did it! Excalibur Academy's eighteenth platoon beat the Military Instruction School's veteran ace, Kaiser Bouffolop! With this, they've scorned one point!"

The commentator's enthusiastic report caused the stadium to erupt into cheers.

"Selia is amazing!" Tessera stared at the screen with rapt attention, her eyes absolutely glittering with excitement.

That really was an impressive display, Arle conceded.

Riselia's sword skills were yet underdeveloped by Arle's and Sakuya's standards. However, her physical prowess when besting the enemy ace was impressive. She'd improved by leaps and bounds compared to when they'd fought together in the Sixth Assault Garden, Alexandria.

"Heh! And the one to defeat Kaiser was none other than Riselia Crystalia! Such a performance befits my worthy rival!"

"...Miss Fenris, please stop hijacking the commentary."

"Ah, what are you doing?! I am not at all done yet!"

◆

"You did it, Lady Selia!" Regina gave her friend a high five upon being freed from the net.

Two of the Military Instruction School's competitors had lost their Holy Swords and slunk back into a dark corridor, muttering bitterly all the while. Defeated competitors were to either retreat to a noncombatant zone or stay put until the administrative bureau picked them up.

Incidentally, the Holy Swordsman controlling the Void Simulator had fled.

"But wow, Lady Selia, you moved so quickly out of nowhere," Regina noted, puzzled. A question mark all but popped up over her head.

"W-well...I guess I was just tense because this is my first time participating in the Holy Sword Dance Festival..." Riselia waved her hand in front of her face evasively. She turned to Shary, still in Leonis's form. "I was basically walking around all day with the shadow shackles. I completely forgot about them."

Shary gave a dry cough. "N-normally, I'd expect you to beat opponents of that level with the fetters still on." Truthfully, she hadn't expected Riselia to forget about the shadowy weights.

"Let's go claim that core flag, then." Regina approached the elevator.

"Ah, wait, before we do, we need to inform Sakuya that we eliminated a few from the Military Instruction School's unit." Elfiné connected an Eye of the Witch orb to her terminal and tried transmitting. "That's strange." She cocked her head.

"What is it?"

"I can't get in touch with Sakuya."

◆

The Imperial Standard Time was 11:40.

"That princess really let loose on us. And here I thought we might be able to enjoy this match a little."

A girl dressed in a uniform from St. Eluminas Monastery

chuckled from beneath the rubble of a collapsed building in the Central Garden. Immediately after the match had started, Chatres Ray O'ltriese's Holy Sword destroyed the building the girl and her comrades were using for cover. The attack that followed ended with the fourth choir's utter defeat. It took only ten minutes.

"But my, that princess. Were her Holy Sword to become a Demon Sword, she'd make for a fine sacrifice..."

The girl's red lips warped unnaturally.

However, preparing the Demon Swords was another group's responsibility. Her tasks were to ensure humanity's capital overlapped with part of the Voids' world and to bring the great goddess's voice to all...

Iris Void Priestess was an apostle of the goddess and speaker for the Voids. She was a powerful undead and a high-ranking officer in the Undead King's forces.

"Now then, let us begin the Void Shift."

The dark priestess took out a triangular stone, a Trapezohedron—a fragment of the goddess's soul. The black rock that drew in the surrounding light floated in the air. It was set almost directly in the middle of the Central Garden, right above the two mana furnaces that were the heart of the Eighth Assault Garden.

Mana furnaces—most people didn't know the secret behind those endless energy sources, that they drew power from the remnants of fallen gods.

Of the two in the Eighth Assault Garden, one housed the remains of an ordinary demigod, while the other held a deity from another world. Which meant that mana furnace possessed a *pseudo-ability to traverse dimensions.*

"Considering it's merely a copy of the Azure Hold, it's quite inferior to the genuine article. But even an imitation of the magical apparatus bequeathed by the goddess is far too great a gift for mere humans..."

The Trapezohedron floating in midair shone dark, resonating. It was beginning to synchronize with the second mana furnace.

"Now, let the ritual begin. Tear away the veil of this false world to reveal true reality. Let this city, the final citadel of humanity, be the beginning of it all."

Crack.

Fissures ran through the air around the Trapezohedron.

"Hee-hee-hee... Hee-hee-hee, hee-hee-hee-hee-hee..."

The Voids were like mere stains that dripped into this world. Those blots alone were enough to drive humanity to near-extinction. But that was only the beginning. A total breach would soon follow. Even the greatest dam needed only the smallest crack to begin its eventual rupture.

A group of shadows rose eerily behind Iris. They were the members of the St. Eluminas Monastery's fourth choir, who'd been defeated by Chatres's attack earlier. They looked up at the Trapezohedron floating in the sky, their eyes hollow and blank.

"Now, let us stoke the furnace fires with our sacrifice. To bring the Void world here."

◆

The Imperial Standard Time was 11:45.

Five figures clad in Excalibur Academy uniforms lay on the ground in Industrial Block III amid the wreckage. These were the Holy Swordsmen of Excalibur Academy's fifth platoon. Unlike the special entry unit, the eighteenth platoon, this squad was made of upperclassman elites who'd handled many Void hive extermination missions.

"Wh-why... Why are we...?" their leader, still conscious, groaned.

They had lost to the Fourth Assault Garden's Academia unit.

Yet based on the fifth platoon's preliminary research, they should have outmatched the Academia's contestants.

"..."

The Academia students looked down upon the defeated Holy Swordsmen with eyes bereft of joy for their victory and pity for their opponents. Their expressions lacked all emotion save reverence for the emptiness.

"Let us stoke the furnace with our sacrifice. To bring the Goddess of Nothingness."

"Now. Let the gates to emptiness open."

They all recited as one, as if they were chanting solemn scripture.

"...Wh-what?! What are you... What are you doing...?!"

Their consciousnesses were linked by a device implanted in their brains. Seraphim, the Phillet Company's Artificial Elemental, was responsible for that. The creature delivered the word of the goddess from the Void world and awakened the power of the Demon Swords in people.

This system, developed by Finzel Phillet, had been tested on the Sakura Orchid's Kenki Gathering.

"With Holy Swords as sacrifices, let emptiness incarnate manifest here."

The Academia unit's members raised their Holy Swords together. No, not Holy Swords. Theirs had already warped into Demon Swords, losing their original characteristics to become blades shaped like tentacles.

The Void Shift project was an effort meant to transport Camelot into the Void world. And it was this squad from the Academia's role to supply the Demon Swords necessary. Since the power of both Demon and Holy Swords stemmed from the same source, they were excellent bait for gigantic Voids.

This made the Holy Sword Dance Festival, a gathering of

powerful Holy Swordsmen, the perfect hunting ground for collecting sacrifices.

"S-stop! Somebody, help...me...!" the fifth platoon leader's scream echoed in vain.

Knights of the empire were stationed around the Eighth Assault Garden to supervise the event, but they didn't seem to respond to this unusual occurrence. The footage drones buzzing overhead had been hijacked by Seraphim, projecting fake footage to spectators.

The tentacle-like Holy Swords came down upon the leader of the fifth platoon.

"Hey there. Looks like you're having fun. Mind if I join?"

"...?!"

The Demon Swordsmen all turned around in unison at this voice.

At some point, a blue-haired girl had arrived entirely undetected. She wore Sakura Orchid traditional garb over her Excalibur Academy uniform.

"I came because I felt the presence of other Demon Swords like mine."

Sakuya Sieglinde stepped forward, her katana enveloped in lightning.

"A squad from the Fourth Assault Garden's Academia, huh? I suppose Miss Elfiné was right to warn us."

"Who are you? An Excalibur Academy swordswoman, all on her own?"

The Demon Swordsmen surrounded Sakuya cautiously. The girl stopped in her tracks, turned Raikirimaru's blade, and...

"Prepare yourselves, Demon Swordsmen—"

...tore away her eye patch, revealing an eye that shone amber. It was the mystic eye of time, given to her by a Dark Lord.

"—for I am one who hunts Demon Swords."

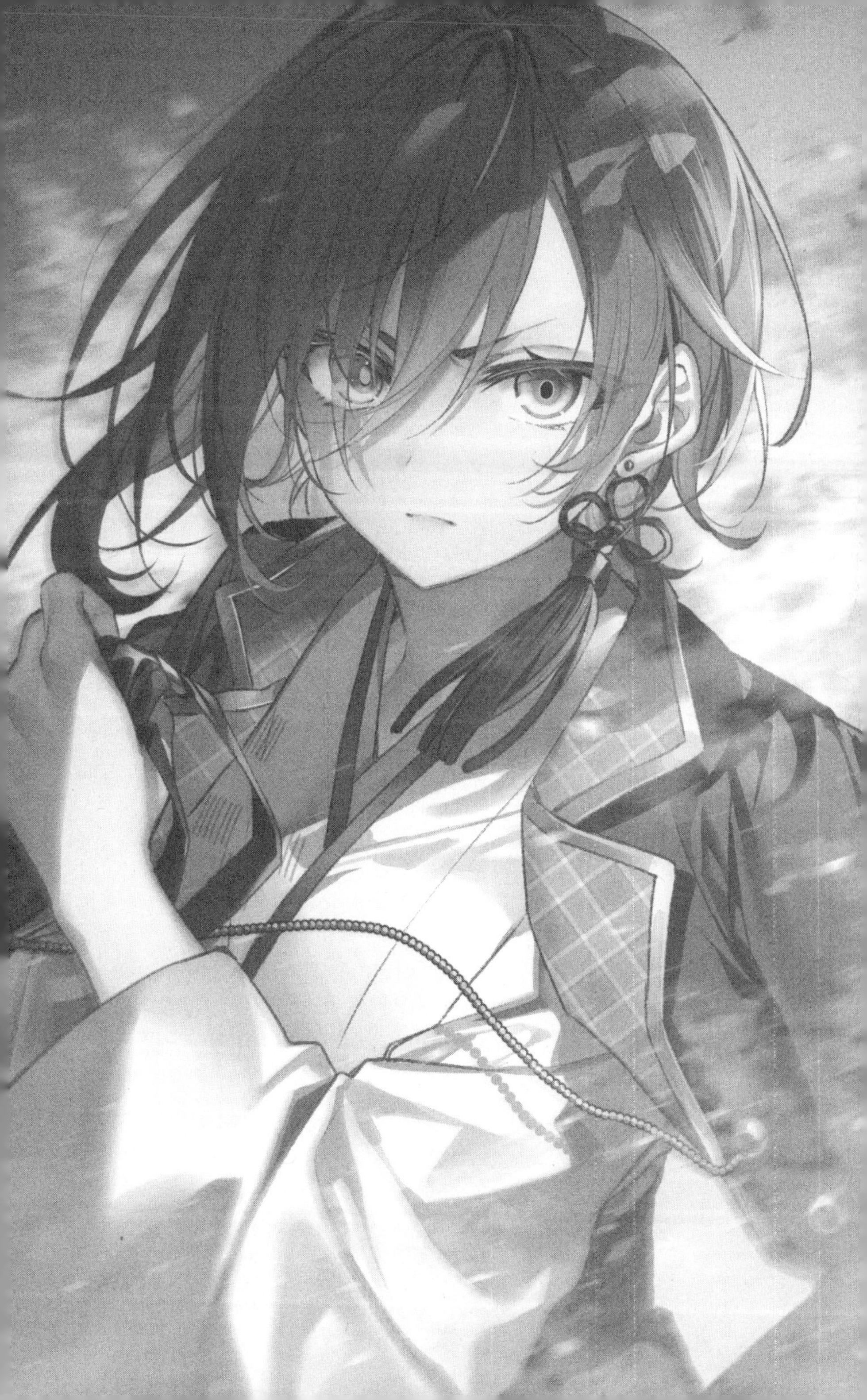

CHAPTER 10

THE SILVER-BLOODED SWORD PRINCESS

"...It's no use. I can't get in touch with her at all." Elfiné shook her head, touching the earring-type communication terminal.

"Maybe she's fighting another unit...?"

"Yes, that's what her terminal readout suggests. As best I can tell, she hasn't been eliminated."

"It's Sakuya. She'll be fine," Regina assured her.

Riselia nodded. "R-right. Sakuya can handle herself." Although she was worried about her friend, Riselia trusted Sakuya.

After eliminating the two Military Instruction School Holy Swordsmen, the eighteenth platoon took the elevator to the second underground level.

"There it is. A core flag," Elfiné said. The Eye of the Witch orb floating in front of her as she led the others down the passage cast its light on a toolbox set on the wall.

Riselia entered their unit code into the toolbox, and it opened, revealing a jewel-shaped object. This was a typical core flag, normally used in practice matches between students.

"And that's our first one. We did it!" Riselia poked it with her finger, and after it read her fingerprint and mana pattern, a point was added to the eighteenth platoon's terminals. "This is where the tough part begins. We have to protect this core flag." She tucked the jewel into a pocket of her uniform.

If another group stole the core flag, the eighteenth platoon would lose half of their accumulated score. In addition to the point from the flag, their terminals also recorded the points they'd received for defeating two Military Instruction School members. Beating Kaiser, the unit's ace, earned more than the other opponent.

"Okay, let's take the elevator to the surface," Riselia decided.

"Yes, I'm worried about Sakuya, too...," Elfiné replied.

It would be harder for other units to discover them if they remained underground, but they'd be overtaken in the race to gain all the core flags. Besides, the Holy Sword Dance Festival was more than just a sports tournament. It was a celebration of the Holy Swordsmen, where each school's representatives competed for their institute's pride. They didn't want to tarnish Excalibur Academy's dignity before countless viewers.

When the eighteenth platoon tried to return to the elevator, Leonis, who'd been mostly silent today, whispered, "Something's coming."

"...?!"

Clang, clang...

The sounds of shrill, metallic footsteps approached rapidly. Red lights illuminated the dark hall.

"Void Simulators?!" Riselia exclaimed, shocked.

"Is it the guy from earlier again?! You should learn when to give up!" Regina fired her Drag Striker, accurately shooting through one machine's segmented leg joint.

The Metahalcum crab-like robot collapsed on the spot, sparks issuing from its internal mechanisms. However, the construct was an anti-Void weapon. Losing a single leg wasn't enough to stop it. It rose again and charged unsteadily.

"...Tch, the elevator's no good. Let's intercept them in the open space out back," Riselia instructed. "Regina and I will guard the back. Miss Finé, Leo, you two go ahead."

"Understood. Leo, come with me." Elfiné pulled Leonis by the arm and ran off.

The Void Simulators weren't much of a threat, but there were too many of them. Anyone who could control so many simultaneously had a top-rate Holy Sword.

The eighteenth platoon fell back toward an open chamber.

"Let's clear them out here!" Riselia raised the Bloody Sword.

Typically, funneling enemies into a narrow passage was the superior strategy, but this area would make using large-scale destructive techniques more feasible.

A loud thud issued from behind Riselia.

"...Huh?"

Riselia and Regina turned around in time to see a partition at the end of the hall close.

"...Miss Finé?!"

No sooner had Riselia called out...

Brr, brr, brrrrrrrrrrrrrr...

...than the ground began to ascend with a loud noise.

"...Lady Selia! This whole place is an elevator for loading supplies!" Regina said, tapping on a nearby control panel with no success.

Riselia bit her lip. The Military Instruction School's Holy Swordsman had chased them here using the Void Simulators then sealed off Elfiné using the partition.

"Take that!"

"Take that!"

"That's for my friends!"

The Void Simulators spoke with mechanical voices.

"Wh-why, youuuuu!" Riselia launched a blade of blood that destroyed a Void Simulator's legs.

"...lia—Selia, are you all right?" Elfiné's garbled voice came through Riselia's earring device.

"Yes, we're fine. How are things on your side?"

"A wall blocked the way, but I opened it with the Eye of the Witch. I guess this was a trap... Or maybe it's better to call it a revenge prank."

The elevator carrying Riselia and Regina continued its steady ascent.

"Miss Finé, at this rate, we'll end up on the surface," Regina explained.

"Understood. Leo and I will head topside, too. Let's regroup at Point F."

"Roger."

◆

"Hahhhhh!"

Sakuya sprinted across the ground, blue lightning crackling under her feet. This was Thunderclap—the peak of her Holy Sword's acceleration power. Each time her sword cut through the air, sparking with pale lightning, a Demon Swordsman fell to the ground.

Her amber-colored left eye shone, allowing her to perceive potential outcomes several seconds before they occurred.

Sakuya could even see seven possibilities at once, using that information to evade fatal outcomes, selecting futures where she defeated her opponents. Merely possessing the mystic eye's power wasn't enough to accomplish this. Instantly knowing which possible result to choose and responding accordingly was a feat beyond a normal swordfighter.

"■■■■■...!"

The Academia squad's Demon Swords let out nondescript howls. Their blades, shaped like disgusting tentacles, twisted like whips to lash at Sakuya. The weapons snapped at her like hungry beasts.

"Too slow. Slow enough for a fly to land on you."

Switching to a one-handed grip, Sakuya pushed herself to move even faster. Cutting down the writhing Demon Swords one by one, she bolted at the Demon Swordsmen directly. The world appeared to stand still around her. Sakuya's perception of time was accelerating.

Is this part of the mystic eye's power?

The mystic eye of time was the perfect companion to Sakuya's Holy Sword. Had the Dark Lord Zol Vadis known of Sakuya's Raikirimaru and its abilities?

Several future possibilities converged into one, sealing fate into certainty.

"Mikagami-style swordsmanship—Levin Slash!"

Sakuya mercilessly cut down a Demon Swordsman.

"...!"

Burning pain shot through her eyeball.

Forty seconds—any more than that and it'll be too much for me...

Sakuya jumped back, cutting down the tentacle-like Demon Swords swiping at her from all directions. The amber glow left her eye, which returned to its natural blue color. Perhaps noticing this change, the remaining three Demon Swordsmen charged her.

"■■■■■...!"

The tentacled Demon Swords fused directly with their owners' arms, moving independently.

"...I see. You've completely discarded your humanity," Sakuya whispered sorrowfully. She gripped Raikirimaru tightly with both hands. "Mikagami-style swordsmanship—Thundering Lightning Slash!"

A tremendous crash accompanied the stroke that cleaved through a tentacle and arm.

That's the third...!

Sakuya transitioned seamlessly into her next attack, felling another Demon Sword behind her, and moving quickly to her next target. As she fought, Sakuya felt an unusual presence and looked up.

"...What?!" Her legs froze up in shock.

A fissure ran through the sky above the Eighth Assault Garden. Cracks formed in reality heralded the arrival of Voids, but this fissure was undeniably different. The air opened wide, like an eye, revealing a world of red.

This irregular tear seemed to peer down at Sakuya without blinking.

No, is that?!

The very same rip in space had appeared over the Sakura Orchid nine years ago.

"■■■■! ■■■■■...!"

The now monstrous Demon Swordsmen howled together. Tentacles shot through the walls of nearby buildings. The monstrous people were evidently content to ignore Sakuya, leaping from wall to wall toward the Central Garden, directly beneath the tear.

"Wait!"

Sakuya immediately activated Thunderclap to pursue.

"...?!"

Crack, crack, crack...!

Unfortunately, multiple fissures formed around her, and repulsive creatures tore through.

"...Voids!"

◆

The large elevator carrying Riselia and Regina slowed to a stop as it reached the surface. Sunlight washed over the pair, forcing Riselia to squint.

"This looks like a storage sector." Regina examined the area cautiously with the Drag Striker in hand.

Box-shaped structures dotted their surroundings.

"We need to regroup with Elfiné and Leo."

"Our rendezvous spot is... Huh?" Regina stared at her terminal in disbelief, then swallowed hard.

"What's wrong, Regina?" Riselia asked.

"Three core flags are moving to this point."

"What?!"

That meant a unit that had already collected core flags was on the move. To have gathered three so soon after the event began meant it was a powerful squad.

"Lady Selia, you don't think—?"

"Yeah. I've got a bad feeling about this."

"Th-the final boss has already arrived."

Riselia and Regina exchanged looks, beads of cold sweat on their foreheads. This was bad. If their terminals detected the approaching core flags, that meant the enemy unit had surely noticed the one Riselia was carrying.

"They're definitely coming this way."

"Let's run for now!"

"Right!"

There was no telling how many people were approaching, but Riselia and Regina doubted they'd be able to handle it on their own. They had to flee beyond the opposing squad's detection range, but...

Whoosh!

...a rippling sound raced over their heads. A giant warehouse had been slashed through diagonally.

"...What?!"

Vrrrrr! Crrrrraaashhh!

The top half of the structure slid over, collapsing to the ground with a great tremor. A cloud of dust rose into the air. The edifice that had stood between the two girls and the approaching threat was gone.

"Lady Selia! That Holy Sword! It's definitely—!"

"I know..."

Riselia spun around, coughing from the dust. She spied a figure approaching from beyond the cloud. A girl in military attire approached slowly, carrying a broadsword-type Holy Sword.

The third princess of the Human Integrated Empire—Chatres Ray O'ltriese. Her dignified jade eyes beheld Riselia and Regina coldly.

"So this is where you've been hiding, Riselia Crystalia. You've saved me the trouble of heading underground."

"Er...Lady Chatres, have I done something to offend you?" Riselia asked nervously.

Chatres shook her head. "No, I bear no ill will toward you. This is a personal issue. Foolish reporters have been hounding me for days, asking my thoughts on Riselia Crystalia and whether I see you as a rival. They even got in the way of my precious time with Altiria. It was truly irritating."

"So you're...venting your anger on me?"

"Yes. Allow me to apologize before we begin. I really want to blow off some steam."

Chatres stopped in her tracks and raised her Holy Sword slowly.

"I will now proceed to overpower you. No one will obnoxiously compare us ever again."

"Sorry about my big sister, Lady Selia," Regina whispered.

"I doubt she'll let us escape." Riselia steeled herself and readied the Bloody Sword. "Regina, keep an eye out for any enemy snipers."

"You got it."

"There's no need," Chatres stated. "My subordinates are not here."

"You came alone, Lady Chatres?"

"Of course. What would be the point of beating you if I had help? The members of the first platoon are keeping watch nearby, so neither they nor anyone else interferes."

It didn't sound like a lie, and Chatres Ray O'ltriese wasn't the kind who resorted to deception. She'd carried three core flags to bait Riselia out of hiding.

Still, this might be a good opportunity.

Riselia glared straight at Chatres. Defeating the strongest, most famous Holy Swordswoman would mean all those core flags, pushing the eighteenth platoon that much closer to victory.

"Regina, cover me!"

"You've got it, Lady Selia!" Regina replied cheerfully from behind.

"Princess Chatres, this might be two-on-one, but I hope you won't think us cowards. The Holy Sword Dance Festival is a team competition, and we're desperate to win."

"Of course, go right ahead. Given the difference in our abilities, this is a suitable handicap for me," Chatres replied seriously before lunging forward.

◆

Chatres closed the distance in a single bound. If Riselia tried to block, her Bloody Sword would undoubtedly shatter. Knowing this, Riselia tilted her blade to intercept the strike.

Claaaaangggg!

The swords locked, spraying sparks into the air. Riselia slid her angled weapon, warding off her opponent's brute strength. The locked blades separated. The two combatants had traded positions.

She's so strong, even after I diffused some of the force. Riselia's hands felt numb.

"Remarkable. It seems I've underestimated you somewhat," Chatres praised her.

"No need to hold back, Your Highness..." Riselia corrected her grip on the Bloody Sword and glared at Chatres.

"That's a good look in your eyes." Chatres raised her Holy Sword overhead. "I'll take this a bit more seriously, then."

The broadsword's blade turned to light, extending to a height of twenty meltes. Chatres's Holy Sword, the Ragna Nova, possessed incredible destructive power. It was capable of slaying gigantic Voids with a single blow, and its astounding range allowed it to eradicate Void colonies from a distance. Chatres could adjust the radiant blade freely.

These were simple abilities, but dealing with them in practice was difficult. Earlier, Chatres had used these powers to blow off the warehouse's roof from a distance. The Ragna Nova was a top-class weapon for dealing with Voids.

Chatres brought her weapon down diagonally. The luminous streak bit through reinforced asphalt easily. Blocking it wasn't an option. Riselia jumped and sprinted up a warehouse's wall. She ran to the top and then launched a surprise attack from above.

"A petty trick!"

Chatres swung the Ragna Nova horizontally, cutting down the warehouse.

"Whoa?!"

Having lost her footing, Riselia nearly fumbled, but she managed to land on her feet.

"Your Highness, they'll deduct points if you destroy buildings!" Riselia called out.

"Getting enough core flags should cancel out any penalties."

"That's a crazy way of looking at it!"

Perhaps that was a quality Chatres shared with Regina.

Riselia's feet stopped. Chatres brought the blade of light up and then abruptly turned, moving her sword as though to block something.

Ting!

A spark bounced off the Ragna Nova—Regina's covering fire.

"Now, Lady Selia!" Regina loosed more shots from far away.

Chatres cut the bullets out of the air, and Riselia used that opening to rush in. The Ragna Nova could change its range freely, meaning that there was no benefit to Riselia keeping her distance from the princess. Her best option was to force a close-quarters battle.

"Hahhhhhhhh!"

Countless blades of blood formed a spiral that converged at the tip of the Bloody Sword.

"Bloody Petal Spiral!"

Chatres watched as a blade of blood erupted before her eyes. The spiral coiled and snaked, moving in a random, zigzag trajectory toward Chatres.

"Enough with the games!"

The Ragna Nova swept the blood blades away entirely. Riselia's attack wasn't over yet, however. She took another step forward, not allowing the princess to back away. Her attack had been a feint to prepare a more powerful strike.

Riselia fought using the same sword style that Chatres did—imperial orthodox. But there was more to it than that. Riselia had studied different schools of technique for years, never knowing if her Holy Sword would manifest. Some of those methods were seen as abnormal, heretical even. In addition to more vicious sword maneuvers, she incorporated kicks and leg sweeps into her fighting, creating a fluid whole.

Normally, Riselia would also employ sorcery to confuse the enemy, but that was out of the question during the Holy Sword Dance Festival. Her fighting style was a blade dance, and it was overwhelming Chatres.

"Your legwork is quite strange for one of the famed Crystalia Knights...!"

"True, this is an unorthodox style—but my soul is still that of a Crystalia Knight!" Riselia shouted, thrusting the Bloody Sword forward.

However, Chatres dodged this full-force attack, albeit only just.

"Fascinating," Chatres remarked, holding up the Ragna Nova. "I'll be the judge of the quality of your soul, then!"

Riselia braced herself, weary of that luminous blade.

"Holy Sword, Mode Shift—Ragna Shadow."

Suddenly, Chatres's Holy Sword shattered. No... It didn't break; it split into multiple fragments.

Chatres swung her Holy Sword down, and all the shards rushed Riselia with deadly precision.

"...!"

Riselia gathered magic in her legs and jumped away, but the razors pursued, their trajectories winding like whips.

Bang, bang, bang!

Sparks burst to life as shards were sent flying back, compliments of Regina's covering fire.

The Ragna Shadow balances both attack and defense. I knew about it from the data, but... Riselia gritted her teeth as she leaped away to evade.

Data couldn't simulate real combat. The Ragna Nova was optimized for eliminating Voids, but its extreme firepower made it too destructive and lethal for use in the Holy Sword Dance Festival, with its many rules and restrictions. It was the same for Regina's Drag Howl.

The Ragna Shadow was tricky, though. These luminous pieces of the blade tracked a target but also acted as a shield to protect

Chatres. In that regard, the princess's Holy Sword was similar to Riselia's Bloody Sword.

Chatres brandished the hilt of her weapon like a whip. The clean strokes from before were gone; now her strikes were constantly shifting trajectories. A flurry of small blades rained upon the battlefield, carving vehicles meant to carry supplies to scrap metal.

She'll overwhelm me if I let her keep me at this range. I have to get at her flank!

Riselia put mana into her legs again, releasing it to propel herself forward. The longer the battle continued, the more Chatres would win out. The gap in their skills was too significant. Riselia needed to settle this fight while she still had mana.

"Bloody Petal Spiral!" Riselia jumped with the Bloody Sword gripped in both hands.

Countless razors of blood converged at the sword's tip, forming a spiral drill.

"Come if you dare, Riselia Crystalia. Mode Shift—Ragna Nova!"

The scattered blades of light coalesced in Chatres's hands again as the princess stood to meet Riselia's do-or-die attack. If they were to clash, the Ragna Nova would overwhelm the Bloody Sword, shattering it.

However...

"Don't forget I'm still here, too. Mode Shift—Drag Howl!" Regina called out.

...the girl's sniper rifle turned into a large anti-Void cannon.

"What?!" Chatres's eyes shot wide.

An intense burst rocketed from the cannon.

Boooooooom!

The target wasn't Chatres herself, but the ground beneath her.

The asphalt caved in immediately, sending Chatres plummeting into the underground passages below. And as the princess tumbled, Riselia delivered a powerful slash.

"Hahhhhhhhhhhh!"

"So this was your plan?!"

"Regina and I don't need a plan to work together!"

They could each understand one another without any special signals. They were best friends and had been raised together since infancy.

The Bloody Sword came hurtling down, blowing the Ragna Nova and Chatres away.

"...!"

The princess's Holy Sword remained intact, though. Chatres landed, braced herself, and immediately corrected her posture.

I put everything into that attack. I can't believe she stopped it...

"I admit it, Riselia Crystalia." Chatres's blond hair fluttered as she fixed her gaze upon her enemy. "You are a Holy Swordswoman worthy of a serious battle." She lifted the Ragna Nova to eye level, and Riselia did the same with the Bloody Sword.

Riiiiiiiiiiiiiiiiiiiiii!

A shrill warning siren blared.

"...?!"

Both women reacted immediately. Every Holy Swordsman knew what that alarm meant—a large-scale Void incursion.

◆

A large creature soared over the open sea, its wings spread and its sizable shadow racing over the waves. It was Leonis's skull dragon.

"...Is it much farther?" Leonis whispered in annoyance as he stood upright atop the dragon's head, watching the horizon.

The skull dragon's flight speed couldn't match a living

dragon's. Such was the result of creating it for fighting, rather than mobility.

The Holy Sword Dance Festival has surely commenced already.

Still, it was too soon for him to give up. He could swap places with Shary halfway through the event.

The skull dragon roared. A large city had appeared in the distance at last.

"There it is!"

CHAPTER 11

RETURN OF THE UNDEAD KING

"A Void attack alarm?!"

Riselia and Chatres both looked up. They saw a tear form in the sky and rapidly expand.

"N-no... A crack that big...," Riselia whispered in disbelief.

"I'm sorry, but it seems our match ends here." Chatres lowered her Holy Sword, a severe expression on her face. She'd looked just as taken aback as Riselia, but only for a moment. "This is an emergency. You two are hereby under my command. We need to regroup with the units from the other schools participating in the Holy Sword Dance Festival, leave this place, and return to the capital to defend the civilians."

"Y-yes! Understood!" Riselia responded.

The two climbed out of the pit formed by the Drag Howl shot and returned to the surface.

"You all right, princess?" a voice asked from Chatres's terminal. "Looks like we've got trouble."

"Colt, I'm joining up with the eighteenth platoon for now. Where are you?"

"The pesky buggers have us surrounded. There's too many of them."

"Any chance you can break through?"

"We're the fearsome princess's first platoon. So long as we have old Balthus and Mifa on our side, we'll kick these monsters' backsides no problem."

"Good, it's reassuring to hear that. Then you should all go assist the other units and head for the Area III coupling bridge. We'll regroup there."

"Huh... Wait, what about you?"

Chatres ended the call without answering. Voids were gushing out of the crack in the sky overhead.

"Damn Voids...," the princess spat. Then she turned to Riselia and Regina. "We'll make for Area III as we return to the capital. Contact your allies while you still can. It won't be long until communications become unstable."

◆

The mana lighting in the underground passage turned red, and a shrill siren howled in the distance. Elfiné pulled Shary, who was disguised as Leonis, by the hand, as they made their way back to the surface.

It looks like the situation took a turn for the worse.

Voids must have attacked the capital.

"Can you hear me, Shary?" a voice called telepathically.

"Yes, Lord Blackas," she replied.

"Those cursed monsters are threatening the kingdom. I am protecting Lord Magnus's school with the three Champions of Rognas, so destroying the monstrosities in the capital falls to you."

"Understood!" Shary replied, forming a copy shaped like Leonis from her shadow.

She let her fingers slip away from Elfiné's grasp and disappeared, swapping places with the decoy.

Let's begin.

Shary returned to her maid-uniformed appearance, held up her Refisca dagger, and vanished into the dark.

◆

Chatres led the charge, with Riselia and Regina following close after.

"Miss Finé...do you read?!" Riselia had tried calling a few times.

"...Yes... I...hear you..."

The transmission finally got through. Elfiné's voice came through Riselia's earring, though it was heavily interspersed with static.

"A gigantic tear in space appeared over the Eighth Assault Garden. Regina and I are under Princess Chatres's command and are heading for the capital as we speak."

"Roger. Leo and I will...the surface...administrative bureau...and then regroup..."

"All right. Be careful out there."

"Yes. You too, Selia."

After ending the call, Riselia quickened her pace to run alongside Chatres.

"Do you have any thoughts, Riselia Crystalia?" Chatres asked, her eyes fixed on the rupture in the sky.

"It looks like the prelude to a Stampede."

"I see. You two have experienced a few of those, after all," Chatres muttered. "So if this is a Stampede, it means a Void Lord is liable to appear."

"Lady Selia, look...!" Regina exclaimed sharply from a few paces back.

Crack, crack, crack...!

A fresh fracture ran through the air directly ahead, and Voids swiftly emerged from within.

"Do we take a detour?" Riselia asked Chatres.

"No, we power through. Follow me!" the princess declared, racing forward as she held her Holy Sword ready.

"Hyahhhhhh!"

The Ragna Nova grew to a length of fifty meltes, and Chatres swiped it through the swarm.

Whooooooosh!

"Wow!" Riselia could only gawk in amazement. If Chatres had brought that power to bear against her, she wouldn't have stood a chance.

"I can't make use of that repeatedly," Chatres confessed, shaking her head. "The larger I make the blade, the more of my power it consumes. We need to break through quickly. Regina Mercedes, cover me."

"Huh?" Regina looked shocked by the order.

"What's wrong?" Chatres questioned.

"Ah, it's just... You know my name...?"

"I know the names of all the Holy Sword Dance Festival participants. As one should."

"Ah, r-right...!" Regina nodded hurriedly.

"Dance, my drenched blade—Bloody Petal Spiral!" Riselia swung the Bloody Sword, cutting down the remaining Voids.

Fly-shaped Voids dove from above, only for Regina to accurately pick them out of the air.

"Hyahhhhhhhhhhhh!"

Chatres forged ahead, cleaving through every foe in her way. Together, the three managed to reach Area III, and from there, they moved to the Central Garden's main street.

"Wait. There's a unit under attack somewhere," Chatres said sharply as she slew a Void standing in her way.

"...?!"

At the very center of a ruined plaza at the heart of the Central Garden was a tear in space that was expanding by the second. Beneath it stood a group of Holy Swordsman, motionless and surrounded by Voids.

"That garb. Are they from the St. Eluminas Monastery?" Riselia wondered.

"Yes, so it seems. Let's help them."

"Okay!"

Chatres raced forward, the Ragna Nova in hand. Riselia kept the pace, deploying a barrier of blood blades... But then she paused. She sensed something amiss.

...?

She had nothing to go on but intuition, yet anxiety gripped her heart. The St. Eluminas Monastery unit surrounded by the Voids... didn't look like they were under attack. If anything, they appeared to be commanding the monstrous things...

Chatres cleaved through the Voids and reached the group first. She knelt by a frightened girl wearing a cassock.

"Are you all right? Are any of you injured?" Chatres inquired gently.

"W-we're fine. You saved us, Your Highness..." The girl looked up with terror in her eyes. "You came at just the right time. I just thought I needed more Demon Swords to add to the pyre."

"...What?"

"Princess Chatres!" Riselia cried.

The girl's red lips twisted into a grin.

"Wha—?"

Slash!

Something akin to spider legs burst from the girl's back, one of which pierced Chatres.

"Khhk... Ahhh...!"

Blood spurted from the princess's body, dyeing her Elysion Academy uniform crimson. Her body was hurled through the air, collapsing hard upon the ground.

"Your Highness!" Riselia shouted in alarm.

A puddle of blood formed beneath Chatres. The girl with the spider legs sprouting from her back looked down on the princess, wearing an ecstatic expression.

"Oh my, my, my! You're so foolish, Your Highness!" The facade of the girl melted away, revealing pale skin, deep red eyes, and a black dress. "How kind of you to offer yourself up as a sacrifice!"

"Hrahhhhhhh!" Riselia lunged with the Bloody Sword.

She had no idea what had just happened, but protecting Chatres was her primary instinct in this situation.

"Heh… Heh-heh-heh…," the woman snickered, blocking the incoming blade at the last second. "Very good. Brave girls are the most delectable."

"…?!"

Clangggg!

The woman arranged the spider legs extending from her back in a pattern reminiscent of a rib cage to shield herself.

"Just who are you?" Riselia demanded.

"Heh. I'm an apostle. A follower of the goddess from the other side of this tear."

"Apostle?"

"Yes. The ninth apostle, Iris Void Priestess."

"Void? You mean this fracture…?!"

"That's right, I opened the gate. Although in truth, I only gave the first push. The real fun is what comes next."

Riselia didn't understand a single word this woman was saying. "Regina, take care of Princess Chatres!" she called over her shoulder while pushing her sword against the spider legs.

"But, Lady Selia, what about you?"

"I'll stall her here. Please hurry. Princess Chatres is a symbol of hope for all the civilians and Holy Swordsmen. We can't afford to lose her...!"

"..."

Regina hesitated for a moment and then bit her lip. "Understood. Please be careful." She hoisted Chatres's limp, bloodied body over her shoulder.

"Oh, I'm not going to let you get away," Iris said before leaping into the air.

"...?!"

An intense mana glow converged in the woman's hand.

"Fifth-order spell—Vars Farga!"

Booooom!

The spell produced a powerful explosion, and a giant pillar of fire erupted around Riselia.

"Ah-ha-ha-ha! Ah-ha-ha-ha! Don't tell me that was enough to kill yo—What?!"

Iris Void Priestess's shrill laughter was cut short. Crimson light—brighter than the flames—emerged. A dress billowed, untouched by the inferno.

"Go, Regina! I'll take care of her!"

After she'd donned the True Ancestor's Dress, Riselia's mana surged furiously.

◆

"You irritating flies. This land will one day be my lord's territory," Shary spat coldly as she threw a dagger.

Hopping from one building's shadow to another's, she slew the insect-like Voids that appeared from the cracks. Landing on a rooftop, she looked up at the giant tear overhead. Voids spilled from it ceaselessly.

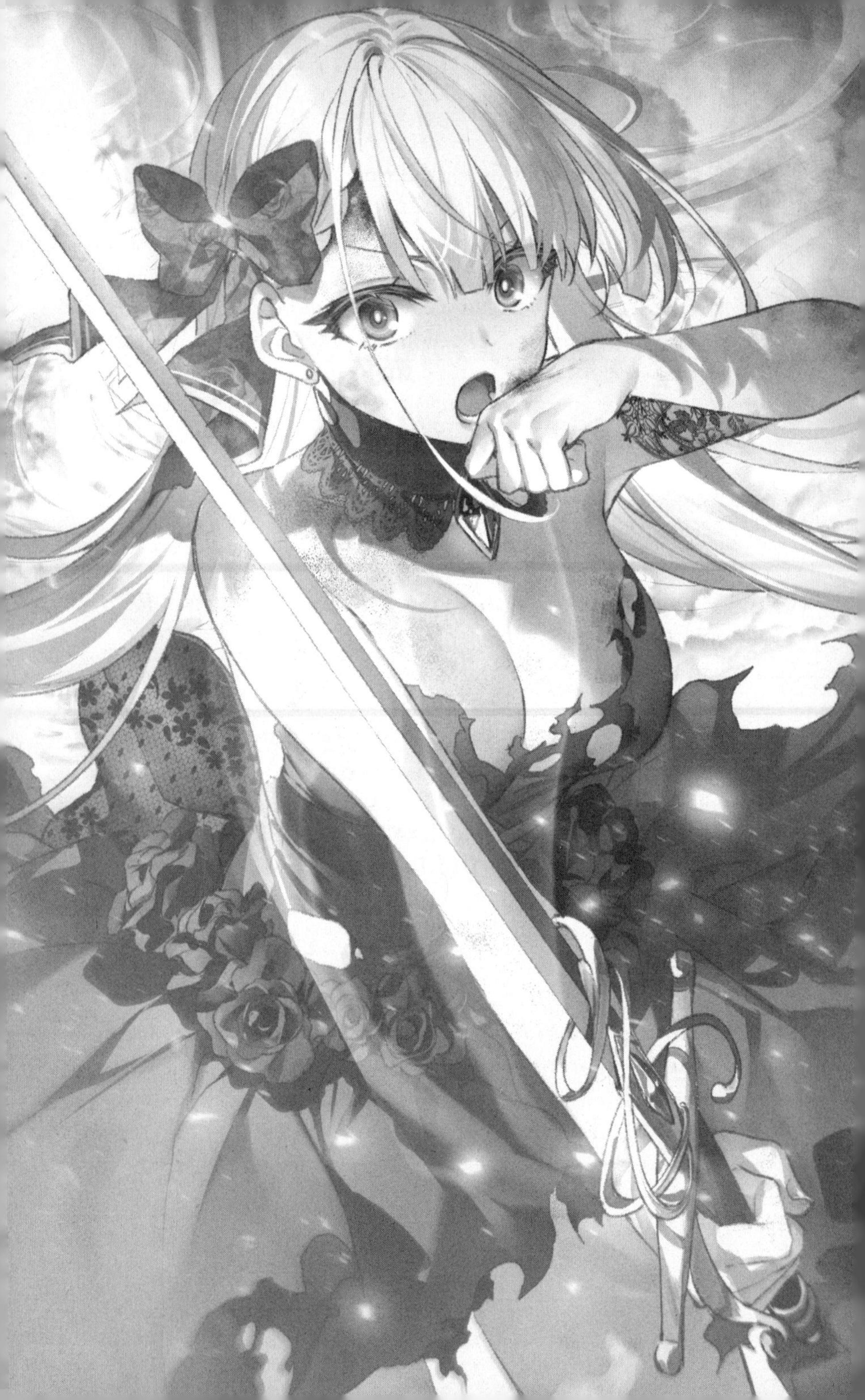

I don't think I'll be able to dispose of that many on my own. Shary bit her lip as she cut down more of the approaching monsters. *Failure to defend my lord's domain after he entrusted me with it is inexcusable. Only death would absolve me...*

And then there was the matter of Leonis's minion, Riselia Crystalia. Shary had to make sure nothing befell her, but locating the girl was difficult in this vast city. And with the Voids radiating intense mana, communication terminals were of no use.

Worst of all, Shary had a terrible sense of direction.

"Seriously, where is she and what is she doing...?" the assassin maid wondered aloud as she swept away a swarm of Voids with shadow whips.

Suddenly, the air over the Eighth Assault Garden was rent in two.

"...What?!"

The rip widened, as if it were being turned inside out, and an ominous red sky spread across the world. From beyond the opening, a gigantic hand appeared.

"Wh-wh-what is that...?" Shary shuddered, her dusk-colored eyes wide with shock.

An unimaginably gigantic Void. Judging by the arm's scale, if a creature of that size fully emerged, it would destroy the First, Seventh, and Eight Assault Gardens completely.

I can't do anything about that thing! Shary's assassin instincts told her that much.

And that was only the beginning.

Crack, crack, crack...!

The tear grew even larger. Two more gigantic limbs reached from the hole.

It...can't be...

Shary's expression turned to one of utter despair. Each of those arms belonged to different Voids. There were at least three of them now.

Shary stared blankly, hopelessly.

"Shary, Blackas! Answer me, I don't care which one of you it is!"

"M-my lord?!" Shary raised her face in surprise after hearing his voice in her mind. *"My lord, you've returned...!"* she replied.

"Not quite yet. I can see the capital, but it'll take me a while longer to return. Shary, inform me of the situation. Things look to be in utter chaos from what I can glean..."

"Yes. A gigantic tear in space appeared over the Eighth Assault Garden, where the Holy Sword Dance Festival was being held," Shary explained while brandishing her whip to fell more Voids. *"Swarms of the monsters called Voids, and at least three gigantic specimens, are attempting to emerge on this side."*

"Hmm. Can you handle them?"

"My apologies, my lord. I cannot do it on my own..."

"I see..." Leonis seemingly took a moment to consider. *"Shary, I give you permission to unleash the Everdark Queen."*

"The Everdark Queen?! But she—"

"We have no choice. We are up against monsters, so our only recourse is to meet this challenge with one of our own."

"But..."

"Do it. Freeing her is dangerous, but I'll manage." Leonis's tone left no room for argument.

"V-very well. I'll do it at once." Shary nodded and removed her maid's headdress.

◆

"Hyahhhhhhh!"

Riselia unleashed the True Ancestor's Dress's power. Her

argent hair shone, and her ice-blue eyes turned crimson. She surrendered herself to the overflowing mana and shot forward.

"Ahh." The spider woman's red lips quirked into a grin, and she snapped her fingers.

The St. Eluminas Monastery Holy Swordsmen turned their blank, emotionless eyes to Riselia and lunged at her together.

She's controlling them?!

Riselia charged into the group. Using the power of the True Ancestor's Dress, she converted her vast Vampire Queen mana reserves into brute strength. She caught a large man rushing her with a high kick to the jaw. Pivoting, Riselia landed a roundhouse kick to another student, knocking him to the ground.

Sorry, but I can't hold back right now!

Riselia brandished the Bloody Sword, producing blades of blood that cut down two more students. She could only hope the wounds weren't fatal as she sprinted for the spider woman.

"Oh my, my. What does this mean?" Iris Void Priestess cocked her head in confusion. *"Why do you have that dress?"* The woman's face lost all expression, but her pupils widened. Vicious malice washed over Riselia, sending chills through her body.

She knows about this dress?!

Did she know Leonis, then? That redheaded girl, Veira, was an old acquaintance of Leonis's. However, Riselia got the feeling that Veira was a friend. This spider woman—Iris—felt different. She eyed the True Ancestor's Dress with a sticky, clinging sort of gaze.

"That garment belongs to a great man. Did you lowly humans ransack Necrozoa's glorious treasure vaults?" Iris scowled and began mumbling to herself. "No, a human couldn't handle that treasure. You couldn't possibly be undead, could you? Lord Nefakess said nothing of the sort—"

I don't understand what she wants, but...!

Riselia moved at lightning speed, swinging the Bloody Sword down.

Clanggggg!

The spider legs deflected her Holy Sword's blade.

"...?!"

"Oh, well. I'll just torture you for information on him. If you're undead, I should be able to hack off your limbs. You won't die so long as your head's still attached, right?"

Iris's arachnid legs came crashing down in succession. Riselia jumped away to evade them, and the sharp limbs crushed the rubble on the ground to bits.

"Bloom wildly, my blades—Bloody Petal Flurry!" Riselia ran in an arc, deploying crimson razors as she moved for Iris.

"Aha!" Iris evaded with surprisingly graceful movements, her spider legs parrying the blood blades. Without the True Ancestor's Dress boosting her strength, Riselia wouldn't have been able to keep up.

Riselia kicked off a building and dashed up its wall. Focusing the mana in her legs, she released it all at once, blasting herself toward Iris.

"Hrahhhhhhhhh!"

She focused all her strength into a single attack, empowering her hands with magic power. The cut severed a few spider legs, sending them flying through the air. However, Iris didn't appear bothered.

"...Were you the one who called the Voids?!" Riselia demanded.

"No, all I did was help open the gate," Iris replied. "The Void monsters are just the vanguard, drawn to this side by the Holy Swords' power."

"What do you mean?" Riselia asked, slashing up to lop off a spider leg plunging for her.

"Just look at that tear in the sky. *The world is being overwritten.*

This world, protected by the Holy Swords, is being overwritten by the great goddess's world of emptiness..."

"...?!" Knocking away a few spider limbs, Riselia risked a glance at the sky.

The rip in space had greatly expanded, and gigantic Void arms were emerging.

They're massive... Are they Void Lords?! Riselia's crimson eyes clouded over with despair.

If they got through, the capital was done for.

"Oh, can you really afford to be distracted?"

Iris opened her mouth and spat sticky threads.

The strands of shining mana bound Riselia's limbs at once, rendering her motionless and pulling her to the ground.

"...Khh!"

Riselia released magical power, hoping to blow the threads away, yet...

Why...?! My mana, it's...!

...the strands only tightened, tearing into the young woman's slender throat.

"Heh-heh-heh. Now, be honest with me, girl. Who gave you that dress?" Iris pressed one of her arachnid legs against Riselia's cheek.

"I'll never...tell you...!" Riselia answered through gritted teeth.

"My, that's a shame... Heh-heh. You bad girl. In that case..." Iris's red eyes glinted ominously. "I'll play with you in my nest until you scream and beg for mercy."

◆

"Lady Selia...," Regina whispered. She turned back to look. Even from afar, she felt the intermittent explosions in her eardrums.

"That's...far enough...," Chatres gasped. "Put me down...here..."

Regina gently lay Chatres's body at the foot of a crumbled building.

"I'll go get a first aid kit." Regina pulled up a map of the area on her terminal, looking for any place with medical supplies.

Fortunately, there was a stand nearby. Regina wasn't sure if places like that were stocked on the incomplete Eighth Assault Garden, but it was worth the attempt.

By some miracle, she did locate emergency treatment materials and hurried back to Chatres. A puddle of dark red had formed under the princess in Regina's absence.

"Your Highness, I'll handle your wounds now. Let me know if it hurts."

"I am a...knight of House O'ltriese... Such pain is...nothing..."

"Don't strain yourself...," Regina said, quickly wrapping a bandage over Chatres's wrist.

Administering medical aid was one of the first things Excalibur Academy students learned. Since Holy Swords with healing powers were rare, knowing how to treat wounds on the front lines was paramount for a Holy Swordsman.

Regina transmitted an emergency request for assistance, but the Stampede made it unlikely that the message would get through.

"What a...disaster... To think an anti-imperial organization infiltrated the Human Church... Were they disciples of the Apocalyptic Cult? What...were they...?"

"Your Highness, please, relax. You'll open your wounds," Regina said, holding the other girl's shoulders.

"...This is pathetic. And I call myself royalty...? The strongest knight? My Holy Sword is meant to defend the people, yet at times like these, I..."

"Excuse me, Your Highness—," Regina whispered before gently wrapping her hands around Chatres's back in an embrace.

The princess's eyes went wide.

"Princess Chatres. Every Holy Swordsman out there looks up to you. You'll go on to lead us all someday. Please, don't say such hopeless things. The entire empire is waiting for your safe return."

"...You talk like you know what it's like to be in my position."

"I apologize if I came across as presumptuous. I'm simply worried for you, Your Highness." Regina released Chatres, a lonely smile on her face.

How could I not worry about my big sister?

Crack, crack, crack, crack...!

Fissures carved themselves into the space surrounding the two.

"Voids?!" Regina stood immediately to protect Chatres, the Drag Striker clutched in her hands.

"Forget about me, Regina Mercedes. Run for...safety..."

Bang!

Regina fired at one of the Voids.

"I refuse. I'll protect you to my last, Your Highness."

Crack, crack, crack, crack...!

The tears continued expanding, with more fly-like Voids spilling out of them.

I might have trouble against so many... Regina felt a cold sweat run down the back of her neck.

She knew it was beyond her to fend off this many alone. The Voids swarmed at her, a loud buzzing overtaking all other sounds.

"...?!"

Just as it seemed hopeless, lightning flashed, and all the Voids rushing toward her fell lifelessly to the ground. Regina saw a familiar white garb flap softly in the corner of her eye.

"I see you need some help, Miss Regina."

"Sakuya!"

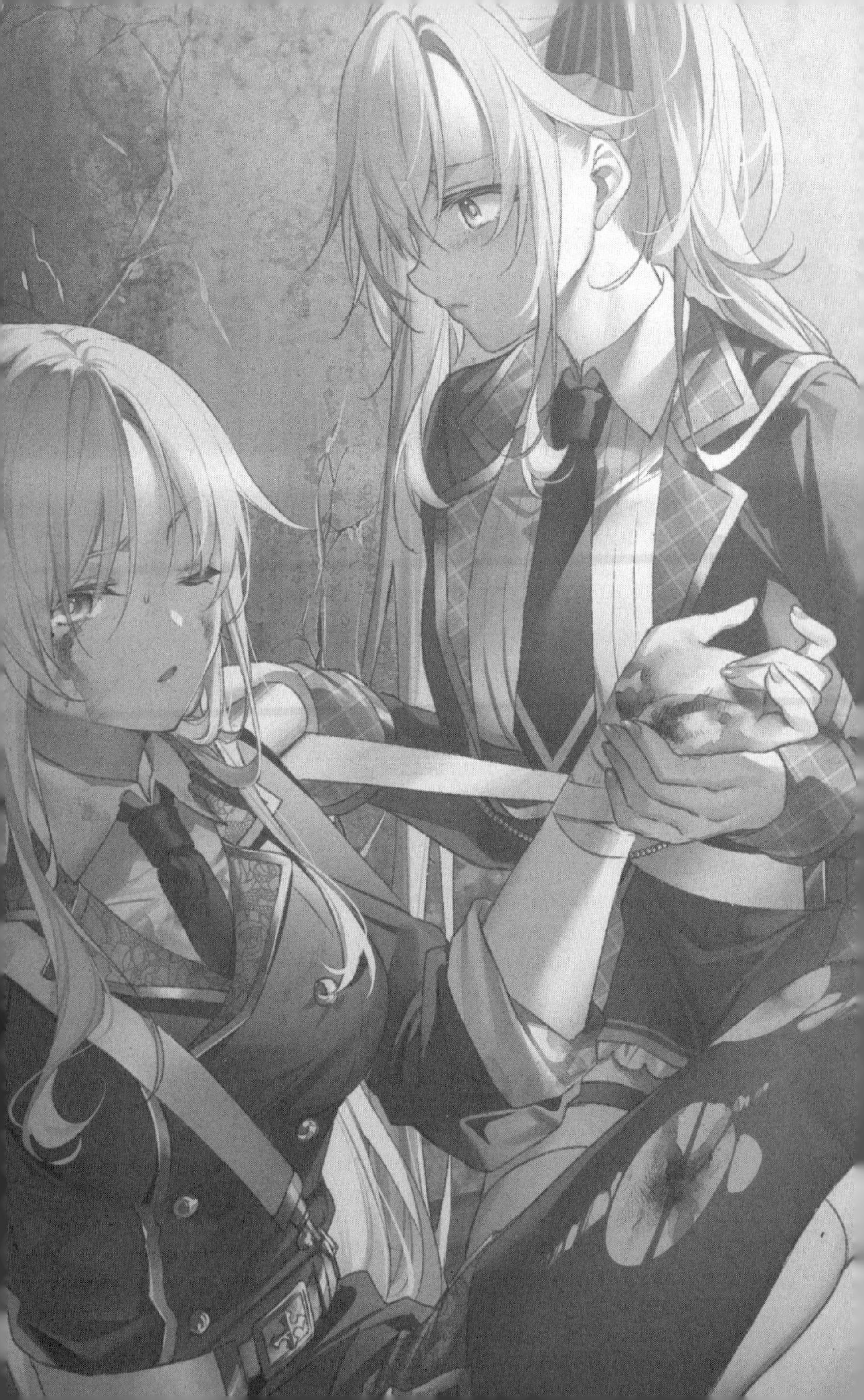

◆

The Everdark Queen, Rakshasa Nightmare, was a devil who reigned over the afterlife, and she was the Undead King's third minion. Long had she been sealed in the Realm Shadows. She was a match for a Dark Lord when her powers were at their full might. Because she took any chance to rebel against Leonis, he'd locked her away.

So while she was his minion, she was also an uncontrollable element. She was, in a sense, Leonis's ultimate weapon. Calling upon her was strictly a last resort.

Shary stood surrounded by Voids, having removed her maid's headdress. The assassin maid closed her eyes and spoke the words that would break the seal.

"First seal released—the lock on the Realm of Shadows has opened."

A small whirlwind whipped up around her, causing her skirt to billow.

"Second seal released—unleash living death upon this place."

The shadow at Shary's feet spread wide, covering the entire rooftop.

"Third seal released—sovereign of the eternal ebon, may your wrath, may your lamentations, fill my hollow vessel."

The shadows consumed Shary's body...

...and the third minion appeared. The personality of Shary Shadow Assassin was wiped away, and in its place emerged the Everdark Queen.

Her body was clad in an ominous dress, as black as a lightless night. Her hands gripped the hilt of the Executioner's Sword, granter of merciful death.

Leonis had given Shary, the guardswoman of the Realm of

Shadows, permission to draw the Everdark Queen into her body. That was the only thing keeping this dangerous entity under control. With Shary's body as her container, the devil's soul was bound and restrained.

Deathly miasma came off her, covering the area. She floated in midair, opening her eyes soundlessly. Their dusk color gave way to a shade of ominous darkness as she beheld the Voids below.

"Bothersome insects," she whispered. "Leave my sight at once."

She gently swung the Executioner's Sword with a single hand, and the swarm of Voids was silently eradicated.

"Is the despicable Undead King not here? Did he flee in fear of me?" the devil wondered in Shary's voice.

She looked around, her attention settling on the gigantic Voids emerging from the tear in the sky.

"I suppose that could prove to be entertaining."

◆

"Ah... Kuh..."

The spider threads dug into Riselia's limbs and neck. As an undead, Riselia didn't need to breathe; however, she writhed in agony regardless, for the strands were draining her mana.

This...is...!

She manipulated her blood blades in an attempt to cut her way out, but the mana-empowered web refused to budge.

"Don't bother. I am a Spider Queen—one of the highest ranks of undead. A lowly undead like you lacks the strength to escape my threads."

Iris Void Priestess let out a resounding laugh. Riselia's mana dwindled, and her consciousness flickered.

"...Ahhh. Ahhhhhhhhhh!" Riselia mustered the last of her

strength, throwing a blood blade at Iris. Yet before it could reach her mark, the liquid razor lost its shape and splashed upon the ground harmlessly.

"Heh. Looks like your mana has run out already."

With her magic power depleted, the True Ancestor's Dress began to fade.

L-Leo...

Although her mind tumbled into the dark, Leonis's face managed to surface. This woman, this monster, was an enemy of humanity who'd summoned Voids to the city. In all likelihood, she was one of Leonis's foes as well, much like that priest, Nefakess.

If Riselia were to fall captive now, Iris would reach her memories and discover the truth about Leonis.

Leo's going to be exposed because of me...!

It was then that Riselia recalled, despite her muddled awareness, how she'd learned to control her mana before the Holy Sword Dance Festival. Shary had trained her to circulate the power while maintaining the True Ancestor's Dress instead of outputting it. At the time, she hadn't quite understood what it meant to do so...

Can I suppress the mana she's trying to steal, instead of just emitting it...?

It couldn't accomplish more than stall for time, but Riselia focused on her heartbeat, pulling in the magical energy her body emitted.

"Oh?" Iris had evidently recognized some subtle change in Riselia and regarded her curiously. "All out of mana already? That was unexpectedly disappointing."

Keep the mana inside my body, as hot as a furnace...!

Suddenly, the True Ancestor's Dress changed—its color turned from bloodred to a shining, pure white.

"What?!" Iris's eyes widened in alarm.

Riselia was surprised, too. Not just with the garment's transformation, but with the way the mana circulating through her body seemed to swell and overflow.

Is my mana being amplified?!

Where had this new energy come from?

With this much strength...

Riselia breathed in. "Hyahhh!" She unleashed all the power running through her at once. Bright light spilled from her body, severing all the threads binding her limbs and neck.

"I-impossible... A low-ranking undead...tore up my web...?!"

Riselia landed on the ground, her white dress billowing. The mana she unleashed was being reincorporated back into her body.

Is this the power of the dress Leo gave me...?

Riselia could tell intuitively that this was the second form of the True Ancestor's Dress—another mode that formed a pair with the crimson one that consumed mana to reinforce her body.

It bolsters the magic power in my body by compressing it. It's a mode specialized for spell-based combat...

Riselia's physical abilities had returned to what they were without the dress, but the sorcerous power within her was growing mighty.

So that training was to help me master this mode.

Raising her Holy Sword, Riselia glared at the panicking Spider Queen. This woman had summoned Voids; she had to be taken alive for information.

"I, Riselia Crystalia, in my capacity as captain of the eighteenth platoon, am placing you under arrest!"

"Heh-heh-heh... You think you can talk down to me, you low-grade undead girl?" Iris began a chant: "Rise forth from defiled soil, you wandering cadavers—Create Undead Army!"

Several dozen magic circles formed around her, and skeleton soldiers appeared from within them.

She summoned skeletons just like Leo!

The newly created warriors rattled as they charged Riselia, weapons ready to strike.

"Come forth, Shadow Wolf Summon!" Riselia chanted a spell, holding the Bloody Sword overhead.

The darkness at her feet warped and changed form, becoming eight ferocious beasts.

Wow! I could only manifest two last time!

The Shadow Wolves sprinted silently, lunging at the undead army.

"Great lord of the undead, beckon flames of darkness to my hands—," Riselia intoned, performing a complicated gesture with one of her hands.

A sphere of black, crackling mana manifested at her fingertips. This was a second-order spell taught to her by the Archmage Nefisgal—the Cursed Flash, Di Farga. It was the most destructive spell in Riselia's arsenal.

"My, my. You wish to challenge a dark priestess with such weak sorcery?" the Spider Queen sneered. She lifted her spider legs. "Great lord of the undead, grant my enemy death and eternal ruination."

A large orb appeared over Iris's head, a sixth-order spell—Vraz Farga. A more advanced version of Di Farga and an offensive spell of the highest caliber.

"Let that great man's spell blow you to bits, giiiiirl!"

Riselia had no chance of winning a clash with a spell far superior to hers. Yet she remained undaunted, fixing her eyes upon Iris and continuing to recite spells.

"Di Farga, Di Farga, Di Farga, Di Farga, Di Farga."

Riselia produced several dozen mana spheres.

"...What?!"

"Di Farga, Di Farga, Di Farga, Di Farga, Di Farga, Di Farga, Di Farga, Di Farga, Di Farga, Di Farga, Di Farga, Di Farga."

Each time Riselia spoke the words, her white True Ancestor's Dress glowed brightly. She wasn't capable of magic above second order yet, but with this vast amount of newfound mana, she could launch a bombardment of lesser spells...!

"You low-grade undead braaaaaaaaaat...!" Iris howled.

Just as Riselia loosed her Di Farga volley, Iris completed her spell, hurling the massive sphere of mana.

Booooooooom!

The Vraz Farga's force was dampened by the many Di Fargas, and it ruptured in the center of the square. The skeleton soldiers and Shadow Wolves were caught in the blast and blown away.

"I'm not finished yet!" Riselia began chanting again.

Each time the magic power circulated through her body, it was compressed, empowering her spells several times beyond their original strength. However, the True Ancestor's Dress's sorcery combat mode had a major flaw—cycling that energy put tremendous strain on Riselia's body. It operated differently from the crimson version, which reinforced physical attributes, making it ill-suited to prolonged fighting.

I can see why she forced me to take basic stamina training.

Riselia pushed her power further, ignoring the pain.

"Very well, then I shall teach you the power of a high-ranking undead...!" Iris Void Priestess tore off her spider legs and threw them into the air. "Take this sacrifice of my flesh, and grant forbidden power unto me...!" The limbs burst into flames and turned into an incandescent fireball. "Eighth-order fire spell—Al Gu Belzelga!"

The burning sphere swelled to a size that dwarfed the Vraz Farga from earlier.

I...can't block this!

Riselia reflexively hurled the Di Farga spells she cast in rapid succession.

"Ah-ha-ha-ha! Don't even bother, it's useless!"

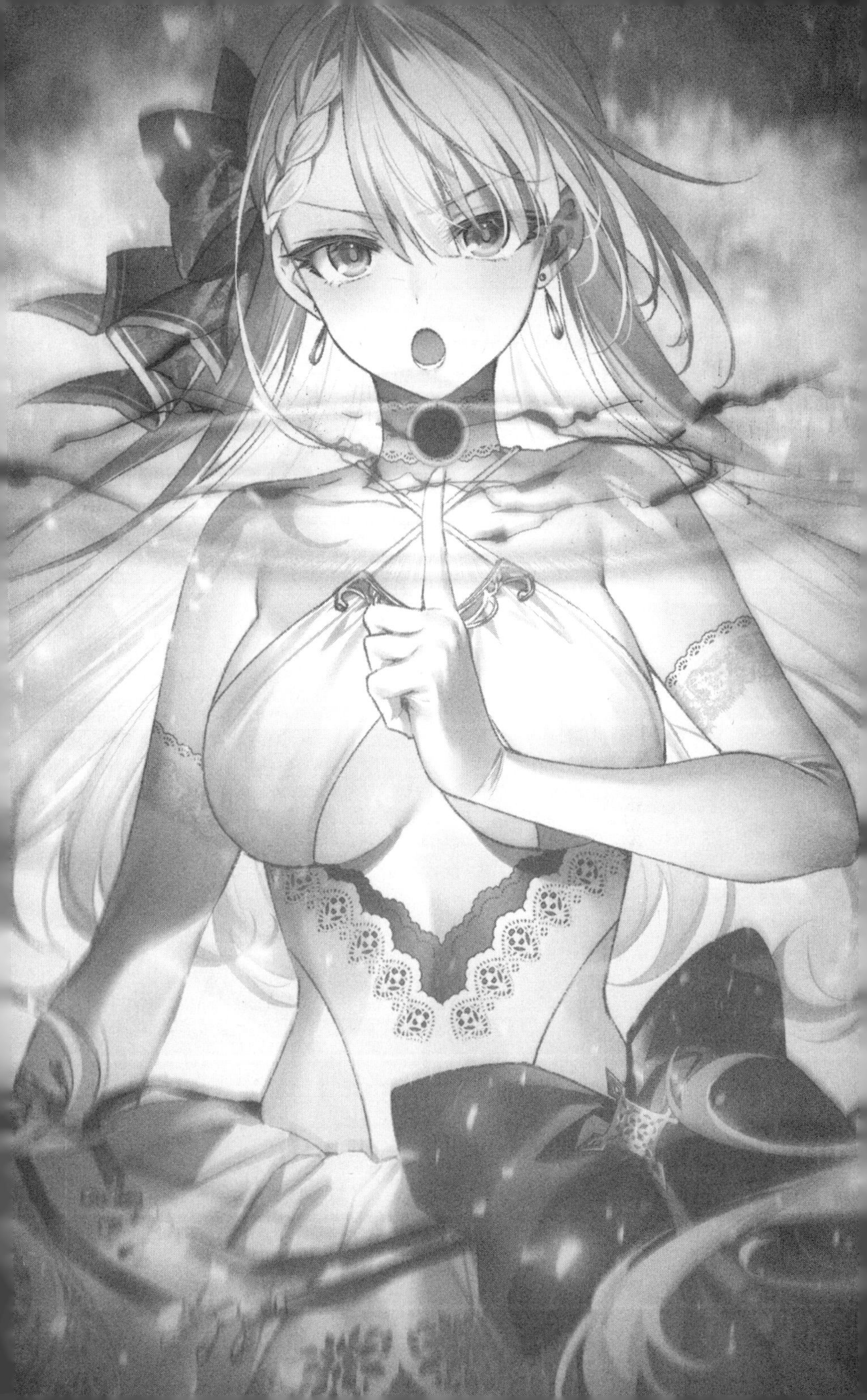

The crimson fireball effortlessly swallowed Riselia's magic attacks.

"...?!"

"Burst—Farga!"

Boooooooooooooooooom!

The explosion didn't manage to reach Riselia. She felt an odd sense of weightlessness, as though gravity no longer applied to her. When she dared to open her eyes...

...Riselia found herself in his arms. He looked right at her—the boy she'd longed to see.

"I'm sorry I kept you waiting, Miss Selia."

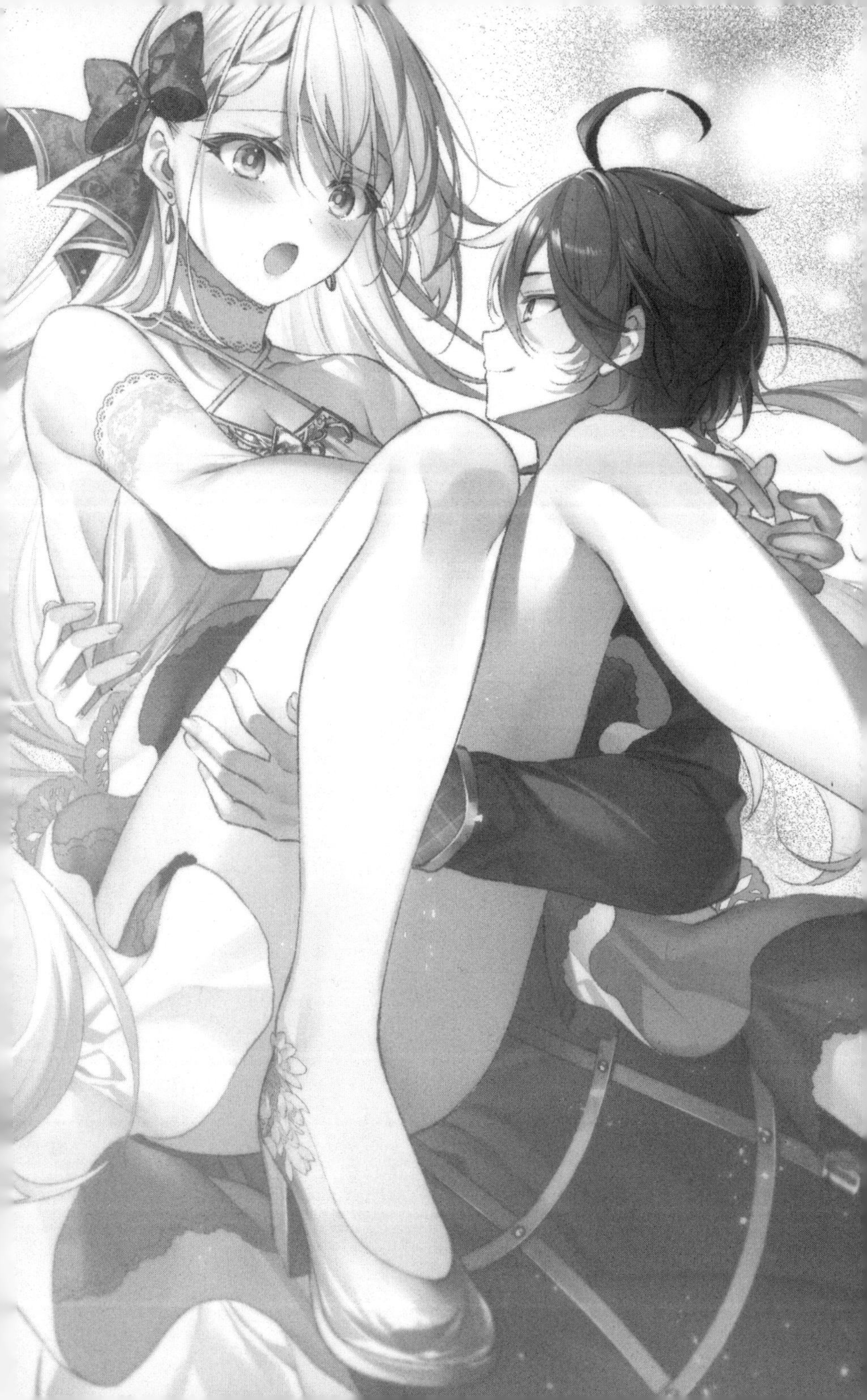

AFTERWORD

Hello, this is Yu Shimizu. Thank you for being so patient. Volume 8 of *The Demon Sword Master of Excalibur Academy* is here for your reading pleasure.

Leonis and his fellow Dark Lords are thrown into another world by the Devil of the Underworld, while the Holy Sword Dance Festival begins in the capital. The apostles plot to enact the Void Shift. Can Leonis return to Riselia's side in time?

Leonis was separated from Riselia and the others in this book, so expect lots of spoiled big-sisterly affection in the next one.

I'm very excited to announce that because of your fervent support, good readers, *Excalibur Academy* is slated for an anime adaptation. Production is already in progress (woo-hoo)! We have an outstanding staff lineup, from the director to the scriptwriters. I hope you're looking forward to it!

Now, for some thanks. To Asagi Tohsaka, thank you for your wonderful illustrations. Riselia is so gorgeous on the cover that I can only sigh in admiration. To Asuka Keigen, congratulations on the fourth manga volume's publication. It's a truly high-quality adaptation, and I eagerly anticipate reading each chapter.

And lastly, the biggest thank-you goes to the readers!

I'll see you all in Volume 9! (And check out the anime when it releases!)

—Yu Shimizu, September 2021